Black Canyon Mystery

Joseph A. Mootz

Living the Dream Publishing
Tucson, Arizona

Published By:
Living the Dream Publishing
PMB 173, 8340 N Thornydale #110
Tucson, Arizona, 85741.

www.livingthedreampublishing.com

ISBN 0-9742080-2-7

Library of Congress Control Number: 2004090409

Second Printing

Published in the United States of America.

Dedication

To my father who introduced me to camping and life in the great outdoors.

To my brother, Pat, who introduced me to the freedom of life on the road.

Disclaimer

The fictional setting of this novel has been closely modeled after the author's own experience at Black Canyon of the Gunnison National Park in Colorado. Certain details of the park have been fictionalized in this work for artistic reasons.

This book has no official or unofficial connection to Black Canyon of the Gunnison National Park, its staff or any park representative. The portrayal of the actions of the fictional characters representing fictional park representatives is not intended to represent any actual representatives. Nor does this portrayal claim to be accurate as to the policies and procedures of the park or the National Park Service.

Gunnison River

Painted
Wall View

Gunnison
Route

South Rim Road

Oak Flat Trail

Visitor
Center

Uplands Trail

Tomichi
Point

Rim Rock
Trail

Park
Entrance

Campground

East Portal Road

Chapter 1

Tommy Atkinson adjusted the small blue nylon pack on his back and turned his gaze towards the dried oak leaves covering the dirt path ahead of him. His dad's hiking boots scattered the leaves as he walked briskly down Oak Flat Trail in Black Canyon of the Gunnison National Park.

The father and son had just left the visitor center where the father had bought Tommy a book on the birds and animals that lived around the canyon. Tommy felt the weight of the book on his shoulders as he tried to keep up with his father on the trail.

He had just turned six years old. His short blond hair hung down over his forehead and his ears. The skin on his face and arms had turned slightly pink from the sun; this in spite of his use of sunscreen throughout the summer in Arizona and on the previous two days of camping and traveling through New Mexico and Colorado. He wore a short-sleeved white T-shirt, a blue nylon jacket, blue pants, and white tennis shoes. His book and a plastic bottle of water shifted awkwardly inside his pack as he walked down the trail.

He wondered where they were going on the hike. They had already got a good look at the canyon from the overlook beneath the visitor center. He remembered leaning over the wooden fence at the overlook and looking straight down into the rocky canyon to the rushing river below. He had gotten scared as he leaned over the railing and jumped back with a jerk when his father put his arm on his shoulder.

His father had said that the canyon was made by the river flowing over the rocks and carrying away dirt for a long time. Tommy wondered where all that dirt was now. There was no sign of it along the steep rocky cliffs that towered above the river.

He remembered asking his dad why there were so many sharp pointy rocks along the stream. His dad had told him that the pointy rocks were harder than the surrounding dirt and were pushed up from the ground when the earth moved sometimes. The softer rock and dirt got washed away by the river and left the pointy hard rocks standing by themselves. Tommy wondered when the earth was going to move again so he could see the rocks being pushed up from the ground.

He continued walking on the trail as it wandered downhill through a dense forest of small oak trees. Tommy thought about his mother. This was the first time he and his father had been away from home since she had died of cancer two months ago. He wondered what cancer was and why it made his mother die. His dad had said that his mother was in a better place now and Tommy wondered if that were true why they had not gone to the better place with her.

A loud screeching sound from the top of one of the oak trees along the trail startled Tommy out of his deep thoughts. He looked up to see a large black bird with a long golden beak, golden feathers on its breast and black and white spotted feathers on its wings. It looked like the same bird as the one on the cover of the book his dad had bought. His dad said that the picture was of a falcon, a bird that ate other smaller birds. Tommy stared up at the tree and tried to imagine the bird trying to catch and eat a tweety bird like that cat always tried to do in the cartoons.

The large bird flew away as Tommy continued down the trail; kicking the dry leaves as he walked down the dirt path. He hoped his dad was not feeling sad over his mom dying. His dad had told him that everyone gets sad after someone dies and that eventually they would be happy again. Tommy hoped that time was coming soon.

Sometimes he felt sad about his mom going away and he did not really understand why she did not come back. His dad said it was all part of God's plan. When he asked his dad what God's plan was, he said he did not know; that no one knows and that we all had to try to be good people and hope God had good plans for us. Tommy wished he knew what God's plan was for him.

The trail curved to the left. Tommy saw his dad walking downhill near the bend in the path. He could smell smoke as his dad puffed on a cigarette as he walked. His mom did not like his dad smoking so much and they used to argue about it a lot. Since she died, it seemed to Tommy that his dad was smoking more than he used to. He remembered him arguing about smoking with a man in the hospital when his mother was sick. The man said his dad's smoking killed his mom, but when he asked his dad about it later he said that the man had lied and was just upset. Tommy still wished his dad would not smoke. Sometimes it made him cough when he had to breathe it when they were riding in their pickup truck.

Tommy could feel his feet moving faster as the downhill grade of the trail steepened. A cool wind blew leaves off of the oak trees and on to the path. He could see dark clouds forming in the distance and hoped it did not rain before they were able to set up camp. He dug his hands deep in his jacket pockets even though he was not cold.

An area void of trees appeared next to the trail and he could see the dark gray walls of the canyons on the other side of the river. Pink stripes of rocks ran up and down the canyon walls. Tommy's dad had told him that the pink rocks melted a long time ago and filled in the cracks in the walls. Tommy wondered what melted the rocks and if they were still soft inside like his crayons were when he left them in the sun in their pickup in Arizona and they melted.

He adjusted the pack on his back and walked down the trail. His dad was farther up ahead of him now. A small bird in the tree above him let out two long loud screeches followed by several shorter sharp cries. Tommy looked up and saw a small blue and gray bird twittering on the branch of an oak tree. He examined it closely hoping that he could remember what it looked like when he tried to find it in his bird book later.

His dad disappeared behind some trees as the trail curved to the left. Tommy tried to quicken his pace and immediately tripped over a tree root sticking out of the ground. He picked himself up and brushed the dirt off his pants. He noticed that his shoe was untied and sat down to tie it. He tried to remember which lace went on top and which on the bottom as he tightly held each piece of string in his hand. He slowly wrapped the laces around each other and formed them into a loose bow. Then he pulled hard on the end strings and tightened the bow down on his sneaker.

Tommy stood up and looked around; his dad was nowhere in sight. He felt a small sense of panic as he hoped his father was waiting for him around the corner. He carefully started walking down the trail again. His dad had taught him that if he ever got lost that he should not panic; he should remain calm and stay on the trail. Tommy knew his dad was just ahead on the trail, but he felt a little scared as he saw the black clouds on the horizon moving across the blue sky towards him.

He reached the bend in the trail and turned towards his left. His dad was still nowhere in sight. The trail continued on for a ways and then turned to the right. Tommy reminded himself not to panic. His dad was just ahead on the trail around the corner, he thought. He walked faster towards the curve in the path.

He followed the trail as it turned to the right and then stopped in anticipation of seeing his dad waiting for him ahead. He looked down the path and saw that it continued downhill in a nearly straight line for a long way. His dad was nowhere to be seen.

"Dad!" Tommy yelled as loud as he could.

The forest fell silent except for the rush of the wind through the trees. Tommy looked at the trail ahead of him and then back the way he came. Both ways looked very similar. He suddenly had trouble remembering which way was the way his dad went and which way was the way he had just come from.

He told himself not to panic. He remembered that his dad said that if he ever got lost he should stay put and stay on the trail until help arrived or he came back to get him.

"Dad, where are you," Tommy yelled. He felt a little ashamed as he heard his voice crack with emotion when he yelled.

A small blue and gray bird in a nearby tree let out a loud chatter. Tommy sat down on the trail and folded his legs underneath him. He took his backpack off and set it in his lap. He wondered how long it would be before his dad came back to get him.

Chapter 2

Johnny Blue drove his red Chevrolet pickup north along Highway 550 just above Durango, Colorado. His friend, Marcie Foster, stared out the window from the passenger's seat. The two good friends were on their way to a relaxing week of camping at Black Canyon of the Gunnison a hundred and fifty miles away.

Johnny had recently retired from his job as an aerospace engineer in Tucson, Arizona. He had spent the summer working part-time as a security guard while building his dream home out of straw bales on his secluded ranch in the desert. He was an average man with an average body and average face. The gray in his hair had recently expanded from just a few patches around his temples to covering his entire head. He caught a glimpse of himself in his rearview mirror and realized that the new look matched his weathered and wrinkled face.

"Looks like a storm blew through here recently," Johnny said.

"I think so," Marcie replied. "The sky looks pretty clear now, though."

"I like driving through these big mountains," Johnny said. "It's nice and green and there is even some snow up on the higher peaks."

"It's pretty," Marcie said.

Marcie Foster's hair was still the same dark brown it had been since she was a teenager, although she would neither confirm nor deny whether it ever had any help staying that color. Only her hairdresser knew for sure. Her silky locks curved from the top of her head around the side of her face and her bangs fell down in front of her green eyes. This was the first time she had allowed herself to relax and take a vacation since her husband had died several years earlier. Since that time, she had kept herself busy running the restaurant they had started along the interstate near their home in southeastern Arizona.

Her restaurant was located near Tucson under the shadow of an oddly shaped mountain known as Picacho Peak. She had met Johnny when he stopped by for dinner on his regular patrol of the nearby state park and aqueduct. He came by a few times a week and told her about his work and the straw-bale house he was building in the desert. Things got pretty exciting for a while when he found two dead bodies in the park and started investigating the deaths on his own.

She was not surprised when he asked her to come along on the camping trip. He had been building up to it for a while and she had thought long and hard about her response. When her husband had died several years earlier, she was crushed and thought she would never get over her loss. She still thought she was not quite over it but recently that old saying "life goes on" kept popping into her head. She slowly began to realize that she needed to go on without her husband and that he would have wanted it that way. She would never get over him and never forget him, but she had to accept her fate and make the best of her situation.

After ten years of hard work she needed some time off. Johnny was a decent man, she thought. They got a long well together and enjoyed each other's company. She was anxious to see the canyon he was always talking about, but mostly she just wanted some time to relax away from the restaurant and her daily routine.

Johnny looked in his side mirror and observed the travel trailer he was towing with his pickup. The small twenty year old trailer had held up well on the trip from Tucson, Arizona to a small campground outside of Gallup, New Mexico the day before. The truck had no trouble pulling the trailer through the mountains and canyons of northeastern Arizona and northwestern New Mexico.

The night before, he and Marcie had spent a few hours around the campfire talking about the events of the last several weeks and getting to know each other better. In the morning they broke camp early. Except for a few high winds knocking the trailer around a little as they drove through the Navajo Indian Reservation in northern New Mexico, the trip had progressed without incident.

They had traveled through the small town of Farmington, New Mexico where the large rock formation known as Shiprock loomed in the distance. They had stopped for gas and lunch in Durango, Colorado. For lunch, they had parked in the local grocery store parking lot and ate sandwiches in the trailer. Now they were preparing to drive through the San Juan Mountains to the town of Montrose and then over to their ultimate destination, Black Canyon of the Gunnison National Park.

Johnny had visited the canyon several times before. It was one of his favorite vacation spots since his wife died in a tragic car accident a few years earlier. He was slowly getting over the loss. He never thought he would get over it, but now something inside of him was telling him to move on. He would never forget his wife, Carol, or how much he loved her and she loved him. He would never forget how they could finish each other's sentences and read each others thoughts.

He would also never forget his son, Jerry, who was only five years old when he was taken away by the same accident. Jerry had just reached that age where he had that ability to perfectly communicate his awe and wonder of the world. Johnny felt like he was just getting to know him when the boy was taken away so violently. He felt a pain in his chest as he thought about the young boy and his insatiable curiosity about the world.

"Looks like they had a fire up there," Marcie said. She pointed to a ridgeline covered with orange and black charred evergreen trees.

Johnny looked up at the ridgeline without commenting. He had heard about the fires that had ravaged Colorado earlier in the summer, but this was the first he had seen of the damage.

"This wasn't the one that was set by that forest ranger burning her ex-husband's love letters was it," Marcie asked.

"No, I think that was over by Colorado Springs on the east side of the Rockies," Johnny said. "I think this was set by someone throwing a cigarette out the window of their car.

"I read in the paper that a woman living in an upscale housing development in this area went a little nuts after this fire and began setting her neighbors houses on fire herself. I guess I'll never understand some people."

"I think we have had enough of fires and upscale housing developments for a while," Marcie said.

"I guess you are right," Johnny said. "I am glad to get away from all that happened over the last couple of weeks after I found that couple on Picacho Peak.

"I kind of miss putting the finishing touches on my house, though."

The truck's engine strained as it pulled the trailer up the steep grade that led into the mountains.

"Do you think the roofers will be done by the time we get back?" Marcie asked.

"As long as the monsoons hold off," Johnny replied. "It should take only a couple of days for them to put up the trusses and then the roof. I am glad I was able to repair the damage to the straw-bale walls before we left.

"I will have plenty of work waiting for me when I get back, but I don't want to think about that now. I just want to relax and enjoy the mountain air."

Great snow meadows blanketed with dry brown grass lined both sides of the road as the couple drove into the mountains. Forests of poplar and white ash trees lined the meadows at the edge of steep slopes covered with evergreen trees. Above the evergreen forests white and gray rocky cliffs stretched for several hundred feet into the clear blue sky. Johnny suddenly felt small; dwarfed by the massive walls that towered above him in every direction.

"Everywhere you look you see something more wonderful," he said.

"I was just thinking the same thing," Marcie replied. She reached over and gently touched his hand on the steering wheel.

The road narrowed and curved its way around steep mountain ridges. The pickup handled the climb well. The traffic was light. Occasionally a sports car caught them from behind and Johnny used the slow moving vehicle turnouts to let them pass. He felt good about the drive. They were making good time and not blocking traffic at all.

He drove the pickup through a narrow tunnel. A large slab of ice lay on the road in front of the entrance to the dark passageway. Water ran off the top of the tunnel and dripped on the windshield as he passed into the darkness. He honked his horn and turned his head towards Marcie who rolled her eyes and smiled.

On the other side of the tunnel, the grade of the road abruptly turned downhill. Evergreen forests lined the steep embankments on either side of the road. Johnny drove slowly through a myriad of sharp turns using his brakes as little as possible. He could feel the trailer pushing the truck from behind. The road wound on for miles and straight stretches were few and far between.

As he negotiated a left-hand curve, a small alpine village came into view a thousand feet below the road. The town consisted of no more than a hundred houses and buildings laid out in the form of a rectangle on the floor of a flat valley. Slopes of mammoth mountains covered with evergreen trees guarded the small hamlet on all sides. Two rivulets of water meandered their way along the muddy bottom of the valley on the outskirts of the town.

"It looks like one of those villages in Switzerland," Marcie said. "It's pretty."

"I'll bet it is really pretty when it is covered with snow in the winter," Johnny said.

He continued driving downhill on the winding two-lane road until he reached the town's city limits. A light blue rectangular wooden sign with dark blue trim identified the town as "Silverton: A Victorian Mining Town."

Johnny parked the truck and trailer in the gravel parking lot surrounding a three story yellow-colored brick building on the outskirts of the town. A large white plastic sign over the building's entrance identified it as the Silverton visitor center.

Johnny and Marcie got out of the truck and each immediately grabbed a light jacket from the cab to protect themselves from the cool air in the shade of the mountains. Johnny walked around the pickup and trailer looking for any unusual signs of wear or other problems to be concerned about. Everything looked in order.

"This is very awe inspiring," Marcie said. She craned her neck to get a better view of the steep pointed mountain tops above her as she walked across the muddy gravel towards the entrance to the building.

Johnny shook his head in agreement.

"Nature is so powerful," Marcie said. "I just can't believe how steep the slopes of those mountains go up intto the sky. They must be several thousand feet above us.

"I bet they don't get many hours of direct sunlight here. The horizon is blocked by mountains on all sides."

"I think you're right," Johnny said. "The sign on the door says we are at about nine thousand feet. I know we still have some eleven thousand foot passes to go over, so some of these mountains are at least twelve thousand feet tall or higher. Kind of puts Picacho Peak to shame."

"Picacho has its own special qualities," Marcie said. She thought about the isolated fifteen hundred foot tall saddle-shaped peak that towered above her restaurant and then caught herself and pushed the thoughts from her mind. She was on vacation, she said to herself.

Johnny reminisced in his mind about the peak that dominated the landscape near his ranch. The peak held a special place in his heart and he was sorry to see the natural wonder tainted by death when two people died of dehydration there while hiking in the summer heat. The experience of finding the bodies and solving the mystery behind the deaths had turned him sour on amateur sleuthing. He wanted to forget all about the experience and relax for a change.

Johnny held the door for Marcie as she entered the building. Marcie was greeted by a woman with white hair, wire-frame glasses, and a flowery blue print dress as she stepped inside. After a brief exchange of pleasantries with the woman, Johnny and Marcie began to browse the full color brochures describing the services the town offered tourists.

"This Durango and Silverton Narrow Gauge Railroad looks interesting," Marcie said. She read from a colorful brochure with the picture of a steam train engine on the front. "It says that you get to travel by a coal-fired, steam locomotive on the same tracks miners and cowboys took over a century ago."

"That does sound like fun," Johnny replied. He read through the brochure and saw that the train originated in Durango and made several daily trips to Silverton and back. "I guess we passed through Durango too quickly. We must have drove right by it."

"It looks like it's an all day ride round trip," Marcie said as she continued to read the brochure. "I think it would be worth it, though."

"Maybe we can take the ride on the way back," Johnny said. "It's too late to make the trip today, besides I am still worried about getting hit by a thunderstorm when we arrive at camp tonight."

He tried to think into the future to the trip back to Tucson. How would they feel about each other by then? The idea of the vacation together was to relax at the park for a few days, but anything could happen. They had no idea what adventures they were in for. Would they be up to an all day train trip together? He caught himself in mid-thought and shook the pessimistic feelings from his head. By the time they passed back through Silverton and Durango, they would probably be closer than ever.

"I am kind of anxious to get to camp too," Marcie said. "Do you really think we'll get hit by a thunderstorm?"

"I'm not sure, but I've been hit by one every time I've visited the park in the past. I am kind of expecting it," Johnny replied. "I guess I'm still not a person that relaxes very well. I like to get everything set up just right before I have any fun."

"I think that is a good quality to have," Marcie said. "We should try to stop in Durango on our way back to Tucson. Maybe we could find a place to camp and take a day to ride the train. We could see the sights and let someone else do the driving."

The couple signed the guest book and thanked the host for her time. They left the building with several brochures in their hands. They assumed their respective positions in the pickup and began the long uphill climb out of town.

The road alternated between lengthy straight stretches and sharp corners along the mountainside. They saw little traffic along the highway as they drove.

Johnny took his time driving; he was not holding anyone up and he enjoyed looking at the scenery.

Although the road was lined with perfectly formed dark green cone-shaped evergreen trees, the mountain peaks above them consisted of bare gray cliffs spotted with light green patches of grass. A stream meandered its way down one of the cliffs as the truck and trailer approached a sharp corner. The foamy white water cut through the dark stone forming several small waterfalls as it meandered its way down to the road.

The evergreen trees became smaller and less dense as they gained altitude. The road was lined with dark gray and red cliffs and the shoulder disappeared completely from the side of the road. Johnny took care to keep his truck and trailer between the lines on the road. Occasionally a small house or mining shack could be seen on the side of the steep mountains. Johnny wondered how they ever got the materials to the site to build in such remote and dangerous places. He imagined what a spectacular view someone would have if they could just find an easy way to reach the buildings.

They traveled over Red Mountain Pass. A sign along the road indicated that the pass was eleven thousand feet above sea level. Marcie could not recall ever being this high above sea level. She had lived most of her life in the Tucson area around three thousand feet in elevation. She and her husband had visited some of the mountains around the Tucson area and even drove to the top of nine thousand foot Mount Lemmon, one of Tucson's more popular weekend recreation spots.

This experience was different somehow. They were at eleven thousand feet, but mountain ranges still towered above them. When they visited Mount Lemmon they were on the highest point for miles around. It was a wonderful feeling to see the desert floor stretch out below her for so many miles, but it was equally wonderful to see the San Juan Mountains rising into the sky above her.

"This is a magical place," she said.

Johnny stared intently at the road and let the comment pass, but Marcie knew he was feeling the same sense of awe and wonder that she felt.

The grade of the road turned downhill and was less curvy. A dense forest of evergreen trees lined the road interspersed with groves of broadleaf trees with light gray bark and light green leaves. The truck and trailer rounded a corner on the road and an array of colorful buildings came into view a few hundred feet below them. The houses in the town were all two or three stories high with sharp angled roofs and painted in blue and pink pastel colors.

"I know this place," Johnny said. "I think the whole town is a historical landmark. They have some hot springs here and I think they even have a community pool set up for people to enjoy them. This might be another good place to stop on our way back."

He continued to drive on the winding two-lane road towards the town. A decorative oval-shaped dark brown sign identified the town as "Ouray: Switzerland of America." A snow covered mountain peak was painted underneath the town's name on the sign which was surrounded by a dense thicket of evergreen trees.

Marcie stared out the window as they passed by several two-story brick buildings and residential houses made of wood. She felt the cool moist air blow on her face as she cracked open her window. She wondered if there were some way to split her time between a place like Ouray and her restaurant in southern Arizona. She liked living in Arizona, especially in the winter with its mild spring-like weather. The heat did not bother her in the summer, but it would be nice to get away from it all in a place with a cooler and moister climate for part of the year.

She felt her attitude towards life changing from what it had been the last few years. She had gotten into a rut. She had a few employees which she considered her family and she enjoyed spending time with them as she worked behind the counter at her restaurant every day. She also enjoyed the interaction with the customers. She felt good about what she did. She felt as if she provided a service that people on the road needed. A lot of her business came from truck drivers who made her restaurant one of their regular stops on the long haul between El Paso and Los Angeles. She had made some friends, but she needed something more.

"I think this town was named after a well-educated Native American leader back in the eighteen hundreds," Johnny said. "Supposedly his name, 'Ouray', means arrow."

Marcie smiled and stared out the window at the small houses as they passed by. She wondered how such an intelligent man with so much knowledge could ever accept a life of solitude in the desert. He certainly loved to share his knowledge when he was around her. Did he have any plan for an outlet of his thoughts and dreams living alone on his ranch in a straw bale house, she wondered.

Johnny continued driving at a moderate speed out of the town of Ouray. The road was straight and rose at only a slight uphill grade. The land around the highway flattened into snow meadows covered with thick dark green grass. He drove past the turnoff for the town of Ridgway and then by the small gently sloped grass covered hills guarding Ridgway Reservoir.

The strain on the pickup's engine eased as he continued driving over the relatively flat road. The air was cool and moist and Johnny felt his hands relaxing on the steering wheel. Occasionally other trailers or recreational vehicles would pass by from the other direction, but no one caught them from behind. They were traveling in the middle of the week and Johnny hoped that the campground would be relatively empty when they arrived. He needed some time to think and there was no better place than a deserted campground on the rim of an awesome-looking gorge.

They drove past a sign advertising the Ute Indian Museum just before they reached the turn off for Chipeta Drive on which the museum was located.

"I guess Chipeta was Chief Ouray's wife," Johnny said. "I stopped by that museum one time. It was quite informative."

"Too bad we don't have time to stop today," Marcie said. "I think the sky looks a little dark to the east."

"Yeah, we better keep moving," Johnny said. "Hopefully the storm will hold off until we can get camp set up."

"I remember reading that Chipeta helped rescue several women and children that had been kidnapped and held hostage by a band of Ute Native Americans during the Meeker Massacre," he said.

"This Meeker character thought of the Native Americans as primitive savages and tried to transform them into God-fearing farmers. When he plowed up their racetrack they killed him and his men and took their women and children hostage for several days."

"I guess Chipeta helped get the women and children back, but then the she and her tribe were banished to Utah along with Chief Ouray. I think he died a few years later in Utah, but she lived on for another forty five years. She remarried and adopted several children after he died.

"When she died on the reservation in Utah she and Ouray were re-buried in Montrose somewhere. I'm not sure where. Maybe we could try to look for their gravesite on the way back."

"You are just a fountain of knowledge," Marcie said. Johnny turned to look at her and they both smiled and laughed quietly.

"That is interesting that she lived so much longer than he did," Marcie said. "And that she adopted children like that. Makes me wonder about what I am doing with my life."

"You are doing a lot with your life," Johnny said. "You bring a lot of sunshine into a lot of people's lives; especially mine."

"Well people in Arizona don't need anymore sunshine," Marcie said. "Besides those people are just passing through. I feel like I need to have more permanent fixtures in my life. I still feel like I am waiting for some kind of great sign to move on and start over again."

"Don't worry," Johnny said. "A sign will come before you know it and you'll be living a life you never dreamed."

Finally they reached the town of Montrose. Johnny drove slowly through the narrow streets of the city stopping for red lights at every signal. He drove past the two story brick buildings and the tree lined parks with Marcie staring out the side window.

"I guess this is the big city," Marcie said.

"This is Montrose," Johnny said. "I think it is the county seat. We are down to about six thousand feet in elevation so you get a good view of some of the mountains in the distance. I guess this is like a crossroads between Denver to the east, Grand Junction to the northwest and Durango to the south."

"It looks like a great place to use as a jumping off point for visiting the mountains," Marcie said.

Johnny stopped at the intersection with Highway 50 and turned right towards Black Canyon of the Gunnison. He drove east through the town's business district.

This part of town reminded him of an old fashioned Main Street, the kind that populated small towns across America decades earlier. The only difference being that this town had been transformed to fit a different economy. The corner drugstore was still present with its blue and orange sign with pink neon lettering hanging off the two-story brick building. A small art gallery with large plate glass windows occupied a single story building directly across the street.

Johnny looked down the street after stopping at the stop sign on the corner. Several of the remaining buildings were boarded up and looked run down. Others were occupied by new and used bookstores, a bank, a tattoo parlor, a tavern and a used clothing store. The small local hospital came into view ahead on the left side of the road.

"That looked like a ranger's pickup parked outside the hospital," Johnny said as he continued to drive. "It looked like one of the white trucks I have seen in the park before. I couldn't make out the lettering on the truck, so I guess it could have been something else."

"Maybe something happened at the park and someone needed to go to the hospital," Marcie said.

"I am sure everything is all right," Johnny said. "Like I said, I am not even sure it was a National Park truck."

The city street turned into a four lane road as they drove out of town. The traffic was still light and Johnny continued to drive at the posted speed limit of fifty five miles an hour. After twelve miles of effortless driving over rolling hills past farm fields and tire stores, they came to the intersection with Highway 347. Johnny made a left turn past the small bait and tackle shop with hand painted signs advertising available products including shotgun shells and ice cold beer.

He drove the truck and trailer up the steep winding road to the park entrance. The road to the park was lined by steep red cliffs and parcels of land covered with green grass and cattle.

Marcie stared out the window at the black clouds on the eastern horizon. They seemed to be speeding directly towards her. She wondered whether they would be able to find a camping spot and set the trailer up before the storm hit.

"Looks like we might get that thunderstorm like you feared," she said.

"Maybe we can unload the trailer and go down to the overlook at the visitor center before it hits," Johnny said. "It is a spectacular view. The dark clouds and lightning will make it that much more spectacular."

The road to the entrance booth looked as if it had been carved out of the middle of the mountain. A grass covered pile of mud and rock towered twenty feet high along the right side of the road adjacent to the booth. To the left side a steep grass covered embankment ran for a thousand feet or more down the mountain. Johnny stopped the pickup next to the drive-up window of the booth. A woman with wavy brown hair wearing a khaki-colored ranger's uniform slid the window open and greeted him with a big smile.

"Where are you folks headed?" she asked.

"Just want to do some camping for a few days," Johnny replied.

The attendant responded by reciting the standard entrance and camping fees and handing him a park brochure. Johnny passed the brochure to Marcie. She unfolded the full color brochure and began to read about the basics of the park.

"How long before this thunderstorm hits?" Johnny asked as he handed the booth attendant the payment.

"Not too long," the attendant replied. "You'll probably want to tie down your trailer pretty good and get inside before it hits. The wind gets pretty rough up here and we usually get some hail too."

"What about you," Johnny said. "Are you going to be okay in this little booth?"

"I'm about to close up," she said. "The ranger running the gift shop had a sudden attack of appendicitis. The only other ranger took her to the hospital. I am going to go relieve him on my way home in Montrose so he can come back and stay the night here."

"We thought we saw a ranger's pickup at the hospital," Johnny said. "I hope she will be all right. So how long will we be left alone without a ranger tonight?"

"The resident ranger should be back within an hour or so," she said. "In the mean time, the campground host will be available to assist you. You'll drive by his site on your way to the campground. He is camped out at the end of loop B."

Johnny thanked her for the information and drove up the road into the park.

"I don't imagine we really need a ranger to camp out in the park," he said to Marcie. "In fact, I don't think I've ever encountered one here except for in the gift shop and entrance booth."

"I just hope the one with appendicitis is okay," Marcie replied.

Johnny drove the pickup and trailer up the small hill past the East Portal Road to the entrance to the South Rim Campground. He made a right-hand turn onto the campground road, drove past the turnoff for the ranger's residence, and then turned left into Loop B of the camp. He drove slowly through the loop while looking for the ideal campsite. Only the campground host's site was occupied. All other campsites were empty.

"Looks like it is pretty slow around here," Marcie said.

"Good," Johnny replied. "That will make it easier to relax and enjoy ourselves."

A cardboard sign with the word "Firewood" hand painted on it hung down from the front of the fifth-wheel trailer in the host's site. Johnny continued to drive slowly on the pavement. At the entrance to the loop, he turned left and started driving through the loop again.

"I think that one on the corner up there looks good," Johnny said. "What do you think?"

"I was thinking the same thing," Marcie said.

Johnny pulled past the corner site and stopped the truck. Both he and Marcie got out to examine the site more closely. After a few minutes of examining the usability of the picnic table and fire ring, they decided that the location would suit their needs.

A gravel area more than large enough to hold their trailer ran deep into the site. The picnic table and fire ring were positioned off to the side of the gravel area. Dense thickets of small oak trees encompassed the site and made for a cozy little setting to view the flat plateau on which the campground was located.

Marcie guided Johnny with hand signals as he backed the fifteen foot trailer onto place on the gravel parking area. Johnny shut off the pickup's engine and walked to the front of the trailer. He disconnected the hitch from the pickup and adjusted the trailer's supports so that it sat level on the ground.

He plugged the trailer's electric cord into the site's outlet and had Marcie check to make sure that the lights worked inside. They both surveyed the surrounding horizon and observed black thunderstorm clouds closing in from the east.

"Are you up to going down to the overlook before this storm hits," Johnny said.

"I think so," Marcie replied. She thought to herself that it might be nice to freshen up first, but she did not want to delay seeing the view either. There would be time to freshen up when they were trapped inside when the storm hit, she thought.

The couple climbed back into the cab and Johnny drove the pickup without the trailer out of the campground. The truck seemed to run much better without its heavy load trailing behind it. He stopped at the pay station near the campground entrance, wrote out a check for two nights stay, inserted it in an envelope, and then deposited the envelope in the pay slot.

"We'll have to remember to put the pay stub on our camp post when we get back," he said to Marcie. He knew the rules clearly printed on the payment envelope required the stub to be put on the post, but he also knew that many campers ignored the rules and either stuck the stub in their wallet or put it on the dash of their vehicle. He wondered why that bothered him so much. Was it because of all the times he started to occupy a space only to find someone else had occupied it and not put their receipt on the post or did he just want everyone to follow the rules like he did?

He drove down the camp road back the way they had traveled when they first arrived. Marcie took in the view of the surrounding area through the passenger's window and could see why Johnny liked visiting here. The flat plateau ran to the west for miles into a blue sky lit up by a bright sun. She could see a crooked gap in the surface of the earth to the east where she assumed the canyon lay. Beyond the open space small hills rose up into the black clouds in the eastern sky.

Johnny made a right-hand turn as he exited the campground and drove downhill towards the visitor center. He drove past the observation point at Tomichi Point. No vehicles were parked at the point's parking lot. He continued driving down the two-lane road on the rim of the canyon towards the visitor center. Marcie caught small glimpses of the canyon as they drove down the road.

A white van passed by from the opposite direction. Johnny and Marcie waved to the gray haired man and woman sitting in the captain's chairs in the front of the van. The reflection of the sky off of the van's windshield made it hard to see if there was any response to their gesture.

Johnny made a right-hand turn into the visitor center parking lot. A single black pickup with a white canopy was parked near the small building built out of peeled logs. The logs were about a foot in diameter and the evening sun reflected brightly off their shiny varnished exterior. The roof of the building was cut at a sharp angle and covered with dark green shingles. An overhang extended the roof several feet past the top of the building's exterior walls.

Johnny parked his red pickup next to the black one and both he and Marcie exited the vehicle. In front of the pickup stood a small out building with two unisex restrooms.

"Now might be a good time to use the restroom if you have to," Johnny said. "None of the restrooms have water, but there is a spigot outside here that you can use to wash your hands and splash water on your face if you need to recover from the trip. I know I do."

"It would be nice to freshen-up," Marcie said.

They each entered one of the restrooms and were greeted by the pungent odor of a pit toilet with its lid open.

A few minutes later Johnny was waiting for Marcie along the log railing overlooking the canyon when she exited the restroom. Johnny held the spigot handle open while Marcie bent over and held out her hands underneath the cool running water. She splashed some water on her face and stood up straight. Johnny handed her a hand towel he had brought from the pickup and she carefully dried her face.

"This mountain air feels good," Marcie said.

Johnny took her hand in his and the couple started walking towards the visitor center.

"Looks like they are closed," he said. "We can go around the side and see the canyon from the rail around the building. Then we can walk down to the observation point."

"Wow, this is spectacular," Marcie said as she approached the rail on the back side of the visitor center."

"It's great," Johnny said. "There is a short trail that goes to that overlook down there. That will really give us a feel for the canyon." He pointed to a flat area surrounded by a fence made out of small log poles and sitting at the edge of a jagged rocky formation jutting out into the center of the canyon.

"I did not realize it was after six already and the center would be closed," Johnny said. "I guess all the campers are hiding out somewhere in anticipation of this storm."

"All except for the ones with the black pickup in the parking lot," Marcie said.

"They must be down at the overlook," Johnny said.

The two walked along the railing to the trailhead. The trailhead split into two trails. "Oak Flat Trail" was printed in white letters on a dark brown sign next to the trail on the left. Johnny pointed to the right-hand trail as the trail to the overlook and he and Marcie started walking side-by-side down the path lined with small oak trees.

"These trees aren't any bigger than the ones we have back home," Johnny said.

"I have seen palo verde and mesquite trees bigger than some of these," Marcie said. "It must be the altitude that keeps them so small. In Arizona it's the heat, I think."

They walked slowly down the trail stepping on oak leaves, roots and flat stones as they walked. The trail curved around and some of the oak trees reached over their head blocking their view. A wide set of steps made of stone and mortar led down to a flat circular observation point. They walked slowly down the stone steps to the log rail fence surrounding the overlook area. They each paused and leaned on the chest high rail with both arms.

"Wow, this is every bit as spectacular as the Grand Canyon," Marcie said.

She gazed down at the copper and gray colored jagged spires jutting out of the ground two thousand feet below her. The south rim of the canyon, which she was standing on, cast a giant shadow over the spires and the river running past their bases. She could see white water rapids and large boulders sticking out of the dark water as the river wandered through the canyon.

The sun shone brightly on the dark gray walls of the north side of the canyon. The dark stone was intermixed with vertical stripes of a pinkish hue. The walls looked flat and almost vertical in angle from Marcie's point of view. As they climbed thousands of feet above the canyon, some of the walls broke off into pointed tops; others flattened out at the top and formed a large plain which ran for miles in the distance before raising itself into hills and mountains. The plain was covered with dark evergreen trees interspersed with orange colored mud and light green short grass.

Marcie stared at the plain on the other side of the canyon. Dark clouds moved visibly over the area towards the canyon. She felt the wind pass through her light jacket.

"That storm is really coming fast," she said. "I think I felt a few drops land on my head."

"I did too," Johnny said. "I guess we should head back to the pickup before it really starts to come down."

They started up the stone steps that led to the dirt trail they had just walked down.

"I guess the walk back will be a little more strenuous than the walk down," Johnny said.

"I think I am up to it," Marcie replied. "It sure was worth the walk. That view is spectacular. We'll have to come back again."

"Oh yes, we'll come back," Johnny said. "And there are plenty of more sights to see also."

The wind blew through the hair on their uncovered heads and rustled the branches of the oak trees as they walked side-by-side up the dirt path. Marcie put her hand on her head to keep her hair from blowing around. Johnny suddenly stopped on the path.

"Did you hear something?" he asked.

"Just the wind," Marcie replied.

"I thought I heard someone calling," Johnny said. "Let's stop and listen."

They both stood motionless as dried oak leaves swirled around their legs. The sky darkened overhead and the drops of rain began to speckle the dirt path.

"I guess it was the wind," Johnny said.

They continued their hike up the trail. As they approached the trailhead, Johnny stopped again.

"Listen," he said.

And then they both heard it.

"Dad, where are you," the emotion filled sound of a young child's voice reached their ears as the dark sky opened up into a full downpour of rain.

Chapter 3

Johnny directed Marcie to take cover from the rain under the visitor center's roof overhang. Marcie ran under the overhang and began to shake the rain off the sleeves of her lightweight jacket. Johnny ran down the trail past the "Oak Flat Trail" sign into the forest as the rain and wind pounded against his face. Rivulets of water streamed down the trail as the rain continued to pour down.

He stopped and listened for the child's voice again. The trees surrounding the trail made a rustling sound as they swayed in the swirling wind.

"Dad, where are you," the young voice echoed through the wilderness again. It sounded to Johnny as if it was coming from not much farther down the trail.

He walked down the wet path. As he turned a corner to his left, he saw a young boy with a blue backpack walking towards him on the trail. The boy jerked his head back and looked behind him when he saw the stranger standing in front of him. Johnny walked slowly towards the boy.

"I can't find my dad," the boy yelled as he turned back towards Johnny. His voice was hoarse and quivered as he spoke.

"That's okay son," Johnny said. He put his hand on the boys head and rubbed his wet hair. His cheeks were also wet, but Johnny could not tell if the moisture came from the rain or if the boy had been crying. A flash of lightning lit up the sky. The boy shivered and then a loud crack of thunder sounded.

"Where did you see your dad last," Johnny asked. He squatted down so his face was level with the boy's face.

"We were walking down the trail," the boy said as he pointed in the direction he had come. "I tripped and had to tie my shoe and then he was gone. I waited for him on the trail like he told me to do if I got lost, but he never came back for me. I walked down the trail but it was getting dark and raining so I went for help."

"Can you show me where you saw him last," Johnny said. He wanted to get the boy out of the thunderstorm to safety, but he thought it was important to at least check out the area first in case the man was hurt or lost himself.

The boy nodded his head and ran down the trail away from Johnny.

"Hey slow down," Johnny yelled at him.

The boy slowed down and Johnny ran to catch up with him.

"My name is Johnny; what's yours?" Johnny asked.

"Tommy," the boy replied.

"I like that name," Johnny said. The boy smiled.

"This is where I tripped and fell down," Tommy said. He pointed to a root on the muddy ground. A clap of thunder sounded in the distance.

The boy continued to walk down the trail leading Johnny around a bend to the right. Johnny looked around the dense thickets surrounding the path and realized that it would be very easy for someone to disappear without a trace if they left the clear area of the two foot wide path.

"I saw him go around here and then I never saw him again," Tommy said. Johnny could hear the boy's voice crack when he spoke.

Johnny reached inside his jacket pocket and pulled out his handheld Global Positioning System unit. The unit was black with a flat gray screen for display. It was only about five inches long, two inches wide and two inches tall. He had forgotten he had left it in his jacket in case the opportunity arose to record his tracks if they did any hiking.

He turned the unit on and stuck it back in his pocket knowing it would take at least five minutes to lock on to the satellites. He wanted to mark the point where the boy last saw his father. He knew that the unit may have trouble locking on to the satellite signals through the thick clouds overhead, but he hoped that somehow the signals would make it from outer space through the dense atmosphere to the ground.

In the meantime he pulled a notepad out of his pocket. He tore a piece of paper off, wrote the words "last seen" on it, and then attached it to the branch of an oak tree near the spot where Tommy had said he last saw his father.

Johnny looked down the trail and saw Tommy waiting for him near the next bend. The boy waved at him to follow. Johnny walked towards him while searching with his eyes for signs of his father. They rounded the corner and walked halfway to the next bend in the trail.

"I sat down and waited for him here," Tommy said. "I was waiting and waiting and he never came back." Tears streamed down his smooth red cheeks.

"Hey, hey, come on Tommy," Johnny said as he bent down to the boy's level and put his arm around him. "It's okay. We are going to find your dad."

The boy sniffled and wiped his nose with his sleeve.

"Do you want to stay here while I go look ahead on the trail?" Johnny said and then immediately regretted saying it.

"No, don't leave me alone," Tommy said.

"Okay," Johnny said. "Let's just walk a little farther up the trail and then we have to get out of this rain."

Johnny checked his GPS unit. It still had not locked on. He tore off another piece paper, wrote "Tommy waited" on it and attached it to an oak tree branch to mark the spot where Tommy said he had waited for his dad.

They walked down the long straight section of the trail side-by-side. Johnny took Tommy's hand in his own. It felt cold and weak. He wondered how long it had been since the boy had eaten. He wondered how long he had sat in the middle of the trail waiting for his father to return. He wondered what terrors went through his mind while he waited. Johnny's mind wandered back to his own son, Jerry, who had died along with his wife, Carol, in automobile accident a few years earlier.

He thought about the times he and his son had watched the storms pass through the valleys below their house in the Tortolita Mountains near Tucson. Johnny remembered Jerry squeezing his hand tighter with each bright flash of light and loud clap of thunder.

The sky lit up with lightning and Johnny felt Tommy's hand squeeze his fingers tight, just as

Jerry's had years ago. A loud clap of thunder burst through the woods a few seconds later.

"That was pretty close," Johnny said. Tommy shook his head in agreement.

Johnny examined the trail closely as they walked. He looked for signs of footprints leading into the woods, but the rain had washed any loose dirt and debris down the trail covering any tracks that might have been there. There were several places where the side of the trail nearest the canyon, dropped off sharply. Johnny surreptitiously kept a close eye on that side of the trail on the off chance that he might see signs that the boy's father had slipped down the steep embankment.

"What's your dad's name?" Johnny asked.

"Tom," Tommy said. "I'm named after him."

"Hello, Tom," Johnny yelled as loud as he could. The two paused to listen for an answer as the rain began to fall in sheets.

"Dad, where are you," Tommy yelled. They both listened closely but only the sound of the rain slapping against the leaves on the oak trees reached their ears.

They both yelled and listened again. They tried several more times before another flash of lightning lit up the sky. The thunderclap rattled the surrounding area almost immediately after the flash.

"That was a little too close," Johnny said. "We need to get to some shelter, Tommy. We will have to have the ranger come out to help find your dad after the rain lets up."

"I don't want to leave my dad out here," Tommy said. "He might be hurt."

"I know son, but we've done all we can for now," Johnny said. "I am sure your dad will be all right. We have to get to some place that is dry so we aren't sick when he shows up, okay."

Johnny checked his GPS unit. The signal had locked on. He marked a waypoint and for good measure tore off another piece of paper, wrote "last look" on it and attached it to an oak tree to mark the place where they had stopped looking. The two started walking back the way they came as the wind and rain pounded harder against the ground.

"Do you want me to carry you?" Johnny said to Tommy as they walked uphill on the muddy trail.

"No, I can make it," Tommy said.

"Let's run," Johnny said.

They ran up the trail as fast as Johnny thought was reasonable. He stopped at the places marked by the scraps of paper and marked more waypoints with his GPS unit. Johnny ran ahead of him on the trail, adjusting his blue pack as he ran.

The two came out of the woods at the trailhead. Tommy hesitated for a moment when he saw Marcie standing underneath the overhang of the visitor center. Johnny caught up with him and they both ran underneath the roof next to Marcie.

"Look at you two; you are both soaked to the skin," Marcie said as a flash of lightning lit up the sky. A clap of thunder drowned out Johnny's response.

"Let's get in the pickup," Johnny yelled over the sound of the driving rain.

The three walked briskly around to the front of the building. Tommy and Marcie waited under the roof while Johnny unlocked the pickup doors. The rain turned to large hail which stung Johnny's head as he fumbled with the keys. He opened the door and waved for the two to come over as he got inside the pickup.

Marcie quickly led Tommy by the hand through the pouring hail to the passenger's side of the pickup. She boosted him up onto the bench seat and then climbed in herself and shut the door.

Johnny started the engine and turned on the heater full blast in hopes of drying out his and Tommy's wet clothes.

"I want my daddy," Tommy yelled suddenly and then covered his face with his hands and burst into tears.

Chapter 4

Marcie put her hands on Tommy's shoulders and tried to comfort him. She felt the coldness of his rain soaked shirt on her hands.

"We need to get you out of these wet clothes," she said.

"Let me take your backpack off hon," Marcie said as she leaned him forward and remove the pack from his back. "Do you have any extra clothes in here," she asked.

"No, just my book and some water," Tommy said. He sniffled and wiped his nose with his sleeve.

Johnny looked through the rain covered window at the black pickup parked next to him.

"Is that your dad's pickup?" Johnny asked.

Tommy answered in the affirmative.

"Do you have any extra clothes in there?" Johnny said. He had to speak loudly over the din of the hail hitting the roof of the pickup and the noise of the air blowing from the heater.

"My clothes bag is in the back," Tommy said.

"Maybe you can see if the cell phone will work," Johnny said to Marcie. "I think the number to the ranger's office is on the park brochure we got when we came in. I'll go see if I can get into the back of the pickup and get Tommy some dry clothes."

A bright flash of light filled the pickup and a loud clap of thunder boomed as Johnny opened the door and stepped outside. The hail had changed to large drops of rain, but the asphalt parking lot was still covered with small white pellets of ice. Johnny slammed the pickup door shut as the wind blew rain onto the driver's seat. He bent his head down low and ran to the back of the black pickup.

He twisted the handle on the canopy door and to his surprise it opened easily. He lifted the door up and locked it into place above his head. Next he stood on the bumper of the pickup, and then stuck his head inside the dimly lit room. A large red and white plastic cooler sat on the left side of the bed of the pickup, two sets of sleeping bags and pillows were stacked neatly next to the cooler, next to the blankets was a cardboard box marked "camping supplies," next to the cardboard box was a small black metal box with a silver lock, finally next to the lock-box was a small blue duffle bag on top of a larger green bag.

Johnny pulled himself inside the back of the pickup and crawled on his knees to the bags near the front. He took his notepad out of his pocket and drew a diagram of the items in the pickup bed. He wanted to make sure he could return the belongings back to their original place if he disturbed anything. He could hear the raindrops landing on the roof of the aluminum canopy over his head. It was dark inside, but he could still make out the outline of what he assumed was Tommy's clothes bag.

He unzipped the bag, just to make sure, and found clothes that looked suitable for a boy Tommy's age. He zipped up the bag and moved it to the back of the pickup. He looked around to see if there was anything else Johnny might need. He thought about taking the small sleeping bag, but then thought that might send the wrong message. He sincerely hoped that they could find Tommy's dad before nightfall. He climbed out of the pickup with the bag of clothes, closed the canopy door and twisted the handle to engage the metal bars that held the door in place.

Johnny ran back to the driver's side of his pickup; the icy pellets on the asphalt had turned to slush. He opened the driver's door and slid onto the seat. When he was settled in, he asked Marcie if the cell phone had worked. When she answered in the negative, he looked at Tommy. His lips were turning blue and he was shaking.

"Let's get you into the restroom so you can change your clothes," he said. He opened the driver's door again and stepped out into the rain. He stood in the doorway and beckoned Tommy into his arms. Tommy stood up on the seat, bent down to keep from hitting his head on the roof, and walked behind the steering wheel to Johnny.

Johnny grabbed him in his arms, stepped back, shut the pickup door and ran through the pouring rain to the restrooms. He set Tommy down on the wet cement and opened the restroom door for him. Johnny handed Tommy the bag of clothes and asked him if he could dress himself. When he said yes, Johnny shut the door behind him and told him to come out when he was done.

Johnny stood under the overhang of the restroom roof. He hoped the boy's father was all right. He hoped the man had just gotten a little disoriented or lost or was maybe still looking for Tommy. Getting lost in the woods was a tricky thing even on established trails. People had been known to step a few feet off of an established path to relieve themselves and never find their way back.

There had been plenty of recent cases of parents letting their children run too far ahead of them on a trail and then not being able to find them. Those cases usually ended in tragedy with the child's body being found not far from the trail after several days of searching by locals. Occasionally a child would heroically survive in the wilderness and be treated for dehydration and exposure after being found. So far in this case, it was the adult who was lost.

Johnny looked around and noticed a single phone booth in between the restrooms and the visitor center. It was an open booth that provided no protection from the elements. He walked slowly over to the phone and then picked up the black hard plastic receiver and held it to his ear; there was no dial tone. He pressed down and let up on the receiver's cradle several times, but there was still no tone. He walked slowly back to the restroom. He noticed Marcie watching him from the pickup and held out his arms to her in a sign of disappointment.

The door to the restroom opened and Tommy stepped outside holding his duffel bag in one hand and his wet clothes neatly folded in the other. The rain began to let up, but the sky was still covered with dark clouds.

"Everything go all right sport?" Johnny said.

Tommy nodded his head. They both ran to the driver's door of the pickup, Johnny opened it and helped the boy up into the cab. Tommy sat down next to Marcie and held his bag of clothes on his lap. Johnny sat down in the driver's seat and put Tommy's wet clothes on the dashboard.

"Still no luck on the cell phone," Marcie said. "I am getting a 'No Service' message."

"I wonder if that's because of the storm or if there is usually no service in this area," Johnny said. "I don't recall ever trying to use a cell phone when I was here before. The pay phone had no dial tone so there was no way to call out. No problem, we'll just drive down to the entrance booth and see if we can get some help. The rain looks like it is letting up."

He took out his notepad and pen again and began to write on the top sheet of paper.

"What was the number of our campsite?" he asked Marcie.

"B-Seven, I think," Marcie said.

Johnny wrote a note on the pad and opened the driver's door.

"I'll be right back," he said.

He ran to the driver's side door of the black pickup and slipped the note halfway through the space between the top of the window and the door frame. He ran back to his pickup and sat down in the driver's seat.

"I just left a little note for your dad to let him know where you are at in case he comes back before we find him," Johnny said to Tommy. "Don't you worry son, everything will be all right."

Johnny patted Tommy on his knee and backed the pickup out of its parking spot. He turned on the windshield wipers, drove to the parking lot exit and then turned left back towards the park entrance.

He drove uphill on the wet winding road past Tomichi Point. The observation point parking lot was still empty. The sky was clear on the western horizon as the orange sun began to sink behind a range of mountains in the distance.

Johnny drove past the entrance to the campground and made a right turn towards the park entrance. As he passed by the turnoff to East Portal Road, he slammed on his brakes. Tommy and Marcie slid forward in their seats and then looked up at the road ahead of them. It looked as though the entire side of the mountain had slid across the road and down the steep embankment taking the park entrance booth and half the road with it. A twenty foot deep and thirty foot wide chasm had swallowed up the road ahead of them. They were trapped inside the park.

Chapter 5

Black Canyon of the Gunnison National Park is divided into two separate parts, the north rim and the south rim. The south rim, the side Johnny and Marcie were camping on, had only one entrance, a two-lane road that meandered for eight miles along the flat mesa above the gorge. Just inside the park, East Portal Road veered off to the right of the main road and led to the river at the bottom of the canyon. This road was very steep with sharp curves and provided no escape out of the park. The north rim of the park had its own separate access road which was not connected to the south rim. The only exit from the south side of the canyon was now blocked by a raging torrent of mud and water at the bottom of a deep split in the earth.

According to the park's brochure, which Marcie had started reading when they first arrived, the canyon was designated as a national monument in 1933 and as a national park in 1999. The park encompassed fourteen of the forty eight mile long canyon and its lands were designated for preservation under the National Wilderness Preservation System. The designation was meant to protect forever the land's natural conditions and opportunities for solitude. Marcie liked the sound of the phrase "opportunities for solitude," but being trapped in the park with no avenue of escape was not what she had in mind.

She had also read that the reason the canyon was called "black" was because it was so deep and narrow that very little sunlight reached the bottom. At the east end of the park, the river is over a mile an a quarter in elevation; by the time its waters reach the west end, it drops over a thousand feet in elevation. At its highest peak, the south rim is around two thousand seven hundred feet above the river; at East Portal on the eastern edge of the park, the rim is only a thousand feet above the stream. Marcie remembered Johnny saying that the East Portal road was so full of sharp curves and steep slopes that he had no desire to travel down it. He had tried it once a few years earlier and that was enough for him.

Johnny tried to recall his experiences at the park to see if he could figure out another way out. He knew the South Rim Road wound alongside the canyon rim for about eight miles and dead-ended at the Warner Point Nature Trail. He was sure the road ended there. There was a system of trails at various intervals along the road at the top of the rim of the canyon. One of those trails was Oak Flat Trail which connected to other paths that ran from the visitor center to the campgrounds. Oak Flat also connected to an inner canyon trail called Gunnison Route that ran all the way to the bottom of the canyon. He knew that East Portal Road ran down to the bottom of the canyon also, but there was no escape once it dead-ended at the river. In his mind, Johnny could think of no way out of the park.

Johnny, Marcie, and Tommy stepped out of the red pickup and walked to the edge of the separation of the earth blocking the road in front of them. They watched the muddy water flow by at the bottom of the hole as the sun disappeared on the horizon. A small canyon ran for several hundred feet on each side of the road now. It looked to be impassable for any type of vehicle. Even an off-road four wheel drive would have trouble finding a place to cross.

"Don't get too close honey," Marcie said as Tommy tried to lean over the edge to get a better view. She could see large boulders and clods of mud being washed from the side walls of the chasm into the muddy water below.

"I guess we'll have to go see if the ranger is at his residence," Johnny said. "It looks like the booth was demolished and is halfway down the mountain by now." He pointed to remnants of the booth's roof a few hundred yards down the steep slope.

"Let's get back in the pickup and see if we can find the ranger," Johnny said. "Hopefully he got back from the hospital before the slide occurred."

They climbed back into the pickup. Johnny turned the vehicle around in the middle of the road and started back the way he came. He drove past the East Portal turnoff to the entrance to the South Rim Campground. He made a right turn onto the camp road and then another right turn at the sign for the turnoff to the ranger's residence. He drove to the small trailer at the end of the road and stopped the pickup. There was no other vehicle or person in sight. The trailer looked dark and deserted.

"It doesn't look like anyone is home," Johnny said. "I'll better go check anyway."

He grabbed the notepad and pen from his pocket and got out of the pickup. He walked up the wooden steps to the trailer's front door and knocked loudly several times. No one answered.

He held the notepad up against the door and wrote a note explaining the situation and then slipped the note in the crack between the door and its frame. He slowly walked back down the gravel path to the pickup where Tommy and Marcie waited for him.

"I'll bet you two are as hungry as I am," Johnny said. "Why don't I drop you off at the trailer so you can get something to eat and I'll head over to the campground host and see if he can help us out? Maybe he has radio communication with the ranger."

"Sounds good to me," Marcie said. "How does that sound to you Tommy; are you hungry?"

"Yes," Tommy said calmly.

Marcie looked closely at the boy's face. He seemed okay. His eyes were clear and although he was not smiling, he did not seem sad or worried. He seemed to be trying to think through the situation. Marcie ran her hands through his blond hair and wiped the sleep from his eyes.

Johnny drove back to the campsite and let Marcie and Tommy out of the pickup. He waited until the light came on inside the trailer before he drove away. Tommy seemed to be handling the situation well, Johnny thought. He had not said much since he changed his clothes. He was probably tired and hungry. Johnny hoped the boy's father would show up soon. He hated to see him suffer and hated to think of what he might have to go through if his father did not show up soon.

Johnny pulled the pickup up next to the white fifth wheel trailer at the campground host's campsite. He was relieved to see the lights on inside the trailer and a late model pickup parked on the gravel space next to it. The sky was clear above his head and a few stars made their presence known by twinkling brightly in the dark blue sky. The storm had passed. The night air had cooled off quickly and Johnny was reminded that he had not had a chance to change out of his wet clothes. He wondered if Tommy's father had found protection from the downpour.

"Hello, anybody home?" Johnny said loudly as he approached the trailer door.

A gray-haired man with glasses stepped out of the trailer door. He wore a blue and white checkered flannel shirt. His shoulders were slightly bent over and he walked slowly down the steps to the ground.

"Hello there, how are you doing?" the man said as he walked towards Johnny. "Need some firewood after that hard rain?"

"No not that," Johnny said. "I need to contact the ranger; do you have radio communication with him?"

"No, I don't," the man said. "He's not in his trailer? I assumed he got back from taking the gift shop worker to the hospital already. I kind of expected to stop by, but wasn't worried too much about it."

Johnny explained the situation and the man invited him inside. They sat down at the dining room table. The host poured Johnny a cup of coffee and introduced himself as Ken Myerson. He said his wife would be back from the restroom soon.

"Is there any way to get a hold of the sheriff or anyone else in authority," Johnny asked. "We tried to use our cell phone but did not get any service."

"I am afraid you won't out here," Ken said. "We're a little too far off the beaten path. There is a pay phone down at the visitor center, but it has been out of order for a couple of weeks. The ranger reported it to the phone company, but they haven't been out to fix it yet."

"I tried it while we were down there," Johnny said. "I really am sick at the thought of someone being lost out in the woods all night. I have to do something."

"It's too dark to do any searching now. We don't want anyone else to get lost out there," Ken said. "It might be nice if someone hung out at the trailhead for a while to see if the guy comes back or maybe hear him if he calls for help."

"I have to get out of these clothes and get something to eat and then I'll head back over there," Johnny said. "My friend, Marcie, can watch the boy in our trailer. Can you watch for the ranger and let him know what's going on?"

Ken said he would "I don't know where he could be, unless he went down to the East Portal Campground or didn't get back from town before the road washed away."

""The booth attendant gave us the impression he should have been back by now," Johnny said. "But you never know what can happen."

"Maybe he got held up," Myerson replied. "Or he could be in the park somewhere, just not at his trailer at the moment."

"Is there anyone else that might be able to help," Johnny said. "If we could get enough people to stand two-hour watches through the night, we could make sure there is someone there if the guy shows up or calls for help."

"I'll ask some of the other campers when I make my rounds a little later," he said. "Last I checked there were only a couple of people in the campground. I think there are a couple of sites occupied in the tent area in Loop C.

"There's a young guy with a Volkswagen bug and a nice retired couple in a van. They might be able to lend a hand. I don't know if anyone else was out on the park road around the canyon rim that might have got trapped by the road wash out. We may see more campers show up to help."

The door to the trailer opened and a white haired woman entered with a flashlight in her hand. She was wearing a heavy green jacket that came down to her waist. She had on beige slacks and held a slightly damp flower print umbrella in her hand. She held the open umbrella outside the door, shook the water off of it, closed it, and brought in inside with her.

"It is really cooling off out there," she said.

Ken introduced Johnny to his wife Louise and then briefly explained the situation to her.

"Oh the poor boy," Louise said. "He must be terrified. Can we go look for his father now?"

"It's too dark," Ken said. "We can't take the chance on losing someone else." Then he explained to her the idea of getting people to stand watch during the night."

"Yes, we must do that," Louise said. "If you need someone to watch the boy, we can help with that too. Anything we can do, just ask."

"I could use a bundle of firewood for the night," Johnny said. He pulled out his wallet and took out a five dollar bill and handed it to Ken.

"Just help yourself," Ken said. "It's under the tarp there. I'll come relieve you at midnight, if I can't find someone else to stand watch."

Johnny thanked the couple and picked up a bundle of firewood from under the tarp outside of the trailer. He put the bundle of wood in the back of his pickup, sat down in the driver's seat and drove back to his own campsite.

When he arrived at the campsite, he got out of the pickup and walked towards the trailer. He opened the door to find Marcie and Tommy seated around the table in the middle of the small enclosure.

"I know that bird's name," Tommy said. "It's a falcon. I saw one in a tree when my dad and me were hiking."

"Very good," Marcie said. "It's a pair-ah-grin falcon." She sounded out the word slowly and Tommy repeated it back to her.

"My dad said that it eats other birds," Tommy said.

Marcie confirmed that the book said the same thing and then turned to Johnny.

"Dinner is almost ready," she said. She pointed to the boiling pot of hot dogs on the stove.

"And how is our little guest doing," Johnny said.

"Fine," Tommy responded. He looked up at Johnny but did not smile. His leg banged against the wooden door of the cupboard underneath the couch alongside the table.

"Your clothes are still wet," Marcie said.

"Yeah, let me go change them in the restroom and then I'll come back and we'll have dinner," Johnny said. "I put a bundle of firewood in the ring, so maybe we can have a fire later."

"Better take a flashlight," Marcie said. "And don't forget to hold your breath when you get close, right Tommy?"

Tommy smiled and kicked the cupboard door with his legs. When Johnny had dropped the two off at the trailer earlier, they immediately set out to fill some bottles of water at the spigot near the loop entrance. Tommy had wrinkled his nose as they walked by the outhouses and Marcie suggested they hold their breath on the way back. When they got back to the trailer they filled a pan with water and put it on the stove to boil. While they waited for the water to boil, they sat down to read Tommy's book on birds.

Johnny grabbed a pair of pants and a shirt from an overhead cupboard and a flashlight from the kitchen drawer and then left the trailer. On his way to the facilities, he tried to think of what to do next. There was no sense in trying to find the ranger. He could be out on patrol on the road that ran along the south rim or he could be down by the river at East Portal. Johnny told himself that there was no way he was going to try to negotiate the steep and dangerous East Portal Road in the dark. The best thing to do was to stand guard near the trailhead and hope the boy's father showed up.

He picked up the stench from the vault toilets several feet away as he walked on the single-lane gravel trail lined with tall green grass. He held his breath while he took off his wet clothes and put on his dry ones. As he exited the small building, the spring on the wooden door creaked loudly while the sound of crickets chirping filled the night air. He just had to hope that the man would find his way home on his own, find the note on his pickup and come looking for Tommy at his campsite.

When he returned to the trailer, Marcie was setting a bowl of hot chili on the table next to a bag of hot dog buns, a paper plate with cooked hot dogs, and a small bowl of cooked corn. Johnny breathed in deeply and felt his stomach rumbling. He had not eaten since they left Durango several hours earlier.

"All right, chili dogs my favorite," Johnny said. "Do you like chili dogs, Tommy?"

Tommy nodded his head and kicked the cupboard with his feet. Marcie fixed him a paper plate of food and set it in front of the boy. She sat down on the side couch next to the table and Johnny squeezed in next to her.

"Looks like I need to get a bigger trailer," Johnny said.

"After dinner I am going to go check on the visitor center for a while," he said to Marcie. "Maybe Tommy can help you clean up before he goes to bed. He looks kind of tired."

"How would you like to sleep with me on the big bed," Marcie said to Tommy.

Tommy shook his head in a positive direction as he stretched his mouth over the end of his chili dog.

"Looks like you get the side couch tonight," Marcie said to Johnny.

"Yep, I definitely need to get a bigger trailer," Johnny said.

Chapter 6

After he finished eating two chili dogs, Johnny drove back to the visitor center under the starry sky. He had stopped by the campground host's site to inquire about the ranger and Ken Myerson let him know that the ranger had not put in an appearance. The host had, however, found some volunteers to stand watch at the visitor center. He had set up a schedule and provided for someone to relieve Johnny at midnight. Johnny looked at his watch, it was almost ten o'clock.

He drove to the visitor center and parked his truck next to the black pickup in the otherwise vacant lot. Except for the absence of rainwater and hail from the storm, the vehicle and the parking lot looked unchanged since he last saw them.

The yellow outdoor lights under the roof of the center reflected off the windshield of Johnny's truck as he stepped out into the cool night air. He grabbed his flashlight off the seat of the pickup and stuffed his notepad and pen in his jacket pocket. He left his laptop computer on the passenger's seat. He had brought the computer from the trailer, in case he wanted to take a look at the GPS points he had marked on the trail earlier. His immediate concern, however, was to find Tommy's father if at all possible.

He walked past the visitor center to the trailhead and then stood motionless to allow his ears to adjust to the quiet of the night. He could hear the sound of rushing water in the distance. He knew the sound came from the river a few thousand feet below him and felt a little awe at something so powerful as to dominate the environment from so far away. The tree limbs stood still in the absence of any wind. An owl hooted three times from the direction of the oak forest covering the canyon rim. Johnny strained his ears to hear any sign of Tommy's father.

The silhouettes of the small bushes and trees near the trailhead stood motionless against the dimly lit horizon. Johnny moved out of reach of the rays of yellow light from the building. He stood still, allowing his eyes to adjust to the dim radiance of the half-moon on the eastern horizon and the multitude of stars overhead. The outline of the dirt path ran for several yards ahead of him.

He decided to follow the path to where he had marked the location of the last sighting of Tommy's father with small pieces of paper. He took the GPS unit out of his jacket pocket and marked a waypoint in case he got disoriented and had trouble finding his way back to the visitor center. He labeled the waypoint "VC" so he could distinguish it from the waypoints he had hastily marked earlier in the day.

Johnny turned on his flashlight and carefully walked down the trail. He enjoyed the feeling of independence and solitude that came from walking outdoors under the clear night sky. He just wished he was traveling under more pleasant circumstances.

He wondered how Marcie was getting along back at camp. Their attempt to find a way to relax and forget about their day-to-day worries had not started out very well. On the drive through the San Juan Mountains, he had imagined that by now they would be sitting around the campfire relaxing and getting to know each other better. They had known each other for a while and Johnny felt that they had a certain chemistry together, but he knew that you really could not get to know someone until you got them out of their element and spent uninterrupted and unoccupied time together. Now all that seemed unimportant with a young boy missing his father.

He walked down the trail listening closely for any unusual sounds in the forest. After a few feet, he stopped and stood motionless.

"Tom, where are you," he yelled. He stood still and listened. There was no answer.

Johnny walked down the path, shining his flashlight ahead of him as he walked. He looked at the backlit display on his GPS unit and saw that he was approaching the first waypoint he had marked earlier in the day; the one that indicated where Tommy said he tripped and fell. He stopped still again.

"Tom, where are you," he yelled. He strained his ears again and an owl hooted three times. There was no other answer to his call.

Johnny stubbed his toe on a root as he started walking down the trail. He stopped and directed his flashlight to the trees around him. The small piece of paper he had left earlier in the day was still stuck on the branch of the oak tree. He examined the dirt path closely, not sure what he expected to find. Nothing looked out of the ordinary. The trail was clear of any debris except where oak leaves and small twigs lined its outer edges. He walked on.

He gave out another call for Tommy's father, but received no answer. He reached the second piece of paper which marked where Tommy had sat down on the trail to wait for his father. Johnny surveyed the surrounding area and found nothing out of the ordinary. He made another call into the night air and was answered by a light breeze rustling the leaves of the surrounding oak forest. He walked on.

When he reached the third piece of paper that he had left earlier in the day, he stopped and surveyed the area again. The piece of paper marked the spot where he and Tommy had turned around due to the oncoming storm. Johnny noticed a small white object mingled with the leaves and twigs along the edge of the trail.

He bent down close to the object and shined his light on it. It was a cigarette butt. The word "Kent" was printed in green on the filter. The cigarette had only burned halfway down and it did not look as if it had been snuffed out. This meant that someone could have dropped it and the burning ashes fell off when it hit the ground or the cigarette had been extinguished through the use of some kind of liquid such as rain or saliva. Johnny pulled his notebook and pen out of his pocket and wrote down the information about the discovery including the number of the waypoint used to mark its location. He left the cigarette butt where he had found it.

He wondered what he expected to do with the information he had written down. He hoped he was not traveling down the same path he had followed over the last few weeks when he had found two dead bodies in the desert and got in over his head when he decided to investigate the incident on his own. He vowed to let the authorities handle the investigation this time; if there was going to be an investigation and if he could find the authorities. His primary concern now was to find Tommy's father and put the whole incident to rest with a happy ending.

Johnny called out to Tommy's father several more times and waited silently for an answer. Each time the dark surrounding forest stood silent except for the distant sound of rushing water. He decided against going any farther down the trail. For all he knew it could be washed out like the road into the park. He could stumble down a ravine and then there would be two people lost. As the campground host had said, that was the last thing they wanted. He stood in silence for ten minutes before walking back up the trail towards the visitor center. A quick happy ending for Tommy seemed less likely with each passing moment.

After Johnny had left the trailer to stand watch for Tommy's father, Tommy and Marcie put the dirty paper plates and plastic-ware in a garbage bag. Then they walked to the dumpster near the entrance to the campground loop and disposed of the bag and its contents. They stopped by the water spigot and filled up two one-gallon plastic bottles. The camp was quiet. The moon and stars lit up the asphalt road enough so that they did not have to use their flashlight as they walked.

Marcie pointed out the North Star and the Big Dipper to Tommy. He had a hard time recognizing the constellation but then all of a sudden he exclaimed, "There it is. I see it." He pointed to the shape in the sky and giggled with glee.

As they approached their trailer on the way back, a dark figure moved towards them on the road.

"Hello," Louise Myerson sang out sweetly. "Lots of stars out tonight."

She approached Tommy and Marcie and introduced herself as one of the campground hosts. Marcie introduced herself and Tommy.

"How do you young man," Louise said to Tommy.

Tommy reached up for Marcie's hand without replying.

"He's a little tired, I think," Marcie said. "We need to get to bed."

"My husband, Ken, is in bed already," Louise said. "You know he's got to go down to the visitor center tonight."

"Well, we better get to bed," Marcie interrupted her. She took two steps toward the trailer with Tommy holding on to her hand. She did not like the direction the conversation was headed in front of the boy. She had no idea what Louise knew about the situation or what she might say. She did not want to take a chance that she would say something to upset Tommy.

"Let me know if I can help in anyway," Louise said. "Nice meeting you."

"Nice meeting you too," Marcie said. "Maybe we can talk tomorrow."

"Nice meeting you Tommy," Louise said. "Good bye."

Tommy managed to meekly say good bye and then wiped his eyes with his one free hand and let out a long yawn.

"You are tired aren't you?" Marcie said. "I'll help you change into your pajamas and then we'll get you to bed."

They entered the trailer and Tommy changed into his pajamas and climbed underneath the blankets on the bed at the back of the trailer.

"Aunt Marcie is my dad coming back?" he asked as Marcie tucked him in. She had told him he could address her as Aunt and Johnny as Uncle if he wanted to. Her heart really felt for the boy. She thought the best she could do was to let him know that he was not alone and that she and Johnny would serve as his surrogate family until his father came back.

"I hope so," she said. "Do you know about God, Tommy?"

"My mom used to say that God watches over all his children," Tommy said.

"Where is your mom now?" Marcie asked.

"She is in heaven," Tommy said. "She died of cancer and then we had a funeral and my dad said she was going to heaven."

"Oh, you poor boy," Marcie said. "Has she been in heaven a long time?"

"No, just a while before we came on this trip," Tommy said. "Do you think my mom was right about God watching over his children?"

"I think so," Marcie said. "God always knows what's best for us even when we don't know what's best for ourselves. All we can do is ask God to watch over us and help us do what is best no matter what happens. Do you want to ask God to do that, Tommy?"

Tommy nodded his head yes. Marcie led him in a simple prayer to ask God to watch over him and his father and Uncle Johnny and Aunt Marcie.

Tommy yawned and turned his head to the side on his pillow. Marcie slid off the bed, turned off the trailer light and stepped outside the trailer. She was wearing the heaviest coat she had, which was not very heavy since she seldom needed any coat at all where she lived in Arizona. The night air felt cold on her face and hands. She decided to start a fire and wait for Johnny to return.

All was quiet when Johnny reached the visitor center. The light from the visitor center reflected off the windshield of the black pickup. Johnny walked towards the vehicle. He noticed an opened carton of Kent cigarettes on the dashboard. He peered through the driver's side window. The bench seat in the pickup was empty except for a light jacket between the driver's and passenger's area. Johnny tried the door handle, but it was locked. He hoped that Tommy's dad had a second jacket and that he was wearing it wherever he was spending the night.

He walked to the back of the pickup. The canopy door was still closed. He saw no point in rummaging through the items in the back of the pickup. He tried to get himself to stop thinking like someone trying to solve a mystery. His experience investigating the death of the couple he had found dead in the desert had taught him all too well the trouble amateur sleuthing could bring to his life.

Johnny walked back to his pickup and grabbed his laptop computer off the seat. He walked over to the bench outside the visitor center and sat down underneath the yellow hue of the outside lighting. He set his computer in his lap, opened the lid, and then waited for it to display the login screen. When the screen came up, he logged in.

First, he loaded the topographic map software he used to interface with his GPS unit. Next, he connected the GPS unit to the cable dangling from the back of the computer and began the process of downloading the tracks and waypoints from the unit to the computer. After a few minutes, the waypoints and tracks were downloaded and displayed as small dots and lines on a topographic map of the park. The map did not show an outline of the Oak Flat Trail, but the tracks that he downloaded from his GPS unit showed the part of the trail that he had walked down while searching for the missing man.

The tracks showed that he had not traveled very far down the trail. The three waypoints he had marked were close enough together so as to be almost indistinguishable. The curving altitude lines on the map were very close together around the waypoint markers. The lines indicated a sharp drop in elevation in the area around the waypoints. It looked as if the trail ran along the top of a steep cliff. Johnny was not sure what he was looking for and the map did not seem to tell him much.

He brought up the official web page for the park which he had downloaded from the Internet before he left Tucson. He clicked on the link for the south rim trails. The web page described the Oak Flat Trail as being a strenuous two mile hike. It indicated that the Gunnison Route branched off of it not far from the visitor center near a "River Access" sign. The Oak Flat Trail looped around away from the canyon until it reached the visitor center again while Gunnison Route led down to the river at the bottom of the canyon.

Johnny knew that the river was named after John W. Gunnison, a surveyor for the U.S. Geological Survey. Gunnison had surveyed the area as part of the Pacific railroad route in the 1850s. After he had left Colorado, the man and most of his survey party were attacked by a band of Native Americans near the Sevier River in Utah. The bodies of Gunnison and his men were later found to be severely mutilated by the attackers.

The incident had become quite controversial because of charges that a group of Mormons had instigated the attack, but the official investigation concluded that they were not involved and that the Native Americans had acted in revenge for an earlier attack by white men. Johnny understood why the river and its canyon bore the man's name, but he wondered if the surveyor had actually traveled Gunnison Route down to the river a hundred and fifty years earlier.

Johnny tried to digest everything the web page described. He clicked on the link to the Gunnison Route description. The web page said that the trail ran from the Oak Flat Trail down to the river. It said the trail was steep and that an eighty foot chain was provided about a third of the way down the trail to assist hikers in their descent and ascent of a steep gulley. In his mind, Johnny tried to picture the trail and the dense oak trees growing on the side of steep cliffs.

He clicked on the link for the trail map. The map showed the Oak Flat Trail meandering from the visitor center covering a triangular-shaped area with several switchbacks. The Gunnison Route did not appear on the map, but a symbol for an overlook was marked near the area where Johnny estimated that Tommy had lost his father. The Gunnison Route description said it was near an overlook on the Oak Flat Trail. He flipped back to the topographic map and compared it to the map on the park's website. It looked as if Johnny had come within a few yards of the overlook point on his search.

Johnny studied the website map closely. It showed that just before the Oak Flat Trail returned to the visitor center, it intersected with the Uplands Trail which ran back to Rim Rock Trail and the South Rim Campground. The Rim Rock Trail ran along the canyon rim from the campground past Tomichi Point to the visitor center.

Johnny tried to make some sense of the map relative to Tommy's missing father. If Tommy's father stayed on the trail, he had three options: one, he could follow the Oak Flat Trail all the way around back to the visitor center; two, he could leave the Oak Flat Trail near where Tommy had lost him and follow the Gunnison Route down to the river; or three, he could follow the trail around to the Uplands Trail and make his way to the campground.

Neither option seemed plausible owing to the fact that as far as Tommy knew the man did not return to his pickup in the visitor center or show up at the campground. Even if his intention was to follow the Gunnison Route to the river, it seemed unlikely he would start down the steep trail without his son close by.

Johnny thought more about the situation. Unless the man was intentionally trying to abandon his son and vehicle, he either had an accident or met with foul play on the trail which prevented him from calling for help or finding his way back to his vehicle. Johnny could only hope that the man was not seriously injured and that Tommy's nightmare would be over soon.

He closed all the programs he had opened and shutdown his laptop computer. He walked over to his pickup and set the computer on the seat inside and then shut the door and listened. The night was quiet, too quiet. He smiled at the joke and then realized now was no time for joking or smiling.

Johnny walked back to the trailhead area and listened closely. A light breeze rustled the branches of the nearby trees. He turned on the flashlight and walked down the fork in the trail that led to the overlook he and Marcie had visited earlier in the day.

He walked down the stone steps that led to the flat ridge guarded by the pole fence. The half moon threw light gray shadows over the canyon below him. He leaned over the rail and listened to the sound of the rushing river. The canyon took on a mystical surreal quality in the moonlight.

He tried to imagine what it would be like to be such a young boy and lose your father all of a sudden. He had not asked Tommy about his mother yet, but assumed that she had not accompanied the two on their journey to the park. There were no signs in the pickup that anyone but the boy and the father had been inside recently.

He thought about his own son, Jerry, and the feeling of loss he had when he died with his mother in a tragic car accident on the interstate between Tucson and Phoenix. When he died, Jerry was about Tommy's age. He was just as innocent and as curious about the world as Tommy seemed to be.

Tommy was holding up pretty well for a young boy left to fend for himself in the company of strangers. Except for the one outburst in the car, he had not broken down at all. Johnny wondered what must be going through his mind. He hoped Tommy was tired enough to have fallen asleep by now.

"Halloo," a voice echoed through the canyon.

Johnny spun around to face the visitor center on the ridge high above him. He looked up to see the silhouette of a man bathed in yellow light standing under the roof of the visitor center.

Chapter 7

"Stay right there," Johnny yelled towards the silhouette standing at the visitor center.

He began walking up the dark trail that led to the observation point. When he reached the log building, a young man wearing a stained white T-shirt and a red bandanna wrapped around his head greeted Johnny under the yellow overhead lights. The young man also wore torn blue jeans and dirty white sneakers. He looked as if he could be no more than eighteen years old.

He introduced himself as Luke Atkins, shook Johnny's hand and said that the campground host had put him on the schedule to relieve Johnny at midnight. He chewed violently on a piece of pink bubblegum as he spoke. Johnny could clearly see the wad of pink sticky mass as the man opened his mouth wide and then closed his jaw down hard.

Johnny looked at his watch and verified the time. The sound of a pack of coyotes yelping in the distance made him look past the dense forest of oak trees into the black night. He felt tired and knew he needed to get some sleep if he was to be any good the next day.

"It's decent of you to help out," Johnny said. "How long have you been in the park?"

"Just arrived today," Atkins said. "I'm traveling around the country for the summer before I start college next month."

"Where are you from?" Johnny asked. He felt a total loss of energy all of a sudden and wondered if his words were coming out slurred.

"Abilene, Texas," Luke said. "But I am going to go to college in San Antonio starting in September."

"Did the campground host tell you what's going on here?" Johnny asked. His mind was wandering and he could not focus on the conversation. He wanted to get back to the trailer and go to sleep.

"Just that some guy was missing in the woods and somebody needed to keep an eye out in case he returned or yelled for help or something," Luke said.

"I guess he got lost on Oak Flat Trail here," Johnny said. "I marked the places I searched with some pieces of paper on the branches.

"There is no sense going down there until the sun comes up. We just need someone to be here in case he comes wandering back to his pickup. If he yells for help, you might want to come back to camp and get the host or me before you go traipsing off after him. We don't want anyone else getting lost. I'm at site B-seven."

"Is that where you have his son?" Luke asked.

"How'd you know he had a son?" Johnny replied. He tried to think back as to whether he had mentioned Tommy at all. He did not think he had.

"Uh, I guess the campground host told me," Luke said. He looked down at the ground and scraped the cement sidewalk with his shoe and chewed harder on the gum in his mouth.

Johnny looked around the parking lot. He saw the missing man's black pickup and his own red truck, but no other vehicles.

"Where's you car?" Johnny asked.

"I left it back at camp," Luke said. "My VW needs a new muffler and I didn't want to wake up the whole campground."

"How'd you get here then?" Johnny asked.

"I used that trail that runs from the back of the campground to here," he said.

"You mean Uplands Trail?" Johnny asked. "I hope you had a flashlight with you." He tried to remember how far of a walk that would have been in the dark. He decided it was probably a little over a mile and could be traversed in less than twenty minutes.

"Nope, just the light of the moon," Luke answered. "It wasn't any darker than when I was traveling on it when that thunderstorm hit this afternoon."

"You were on the trail this afternoon?" Johnny said. "Did you walk down the Oak Flat Trail too?"

"No, I saw the storm coming and headed back to camp before I reached Oak Flat," Luke said. He stared at the ground and chewed faster on his piece of gum.

Johnny gave Luke his flashlight in case he needed it and reminded him to get help before going off in the woods alone. He stretched his neck from side-to-side and yawned.

"I am going to try to get some shut-eye so I can help with the search in the morning," he said.

Atkins blew a bubble with his gum until it burst over his nose. He sucked the pink elastic substance back into his mouth with a loud slurping sound.

Johnny got in his pickup and drove out of the parking lot back to the campground road turn off. He drove part of the way down the ranger residence's driveway and observed that the trailer was still dark and the parking area absent of any vehicles. He put the transmission in reverse and backed down the driveway to the campground access road. He made a left turn onto Loop B and noticed that the campground host's trailer was also dark and that his truck was still parked in front of his trailer. He drove to site B-seven and parked his pickup in front of his trailer.

As he walked around the front of his truck he smelled smoke from a campfire. He looked around and saw orange flames rising up in the night air above the site's fire ring. Marcie was sitting in one of two black collapsible canvas chairs next to the fire. Her hands were dug deep in her pockets and her chin was resting on her chest.

"What are you doing still up?" Johnny said in his normal loud voice.

Marcie shushed him and held one finger up to her closed mouth. Johnny lowered his voice and asked the question again as he sat down on the chair next to her.

"Just waiting to make sure you got home all right," she whispered.

Johnny reached over and patted her left hand which was resting on her leg. The air from the fire felt hot against his face. A loud popping sound came from the fire ring and several sparks flew up in the air above the burning logs. Johnny watched the sparks as they floated above the dark silhouettes of the surrounding trees and then disappeared into the starry sky. A slight breeze blew smoke from the fire away from him.

"How is little Tommy doing?" Johnny asked. His energy had come back to him and he forgot about going to bed.

"He went right to sleep after we cleaned up," she said. "I think the day really wore him out." She felt tired, but was glad to have some company and glad to see Johnny back safely.

"I'd be worn out too, if I went through what he went through today," Johnny said. "He's a real trooper."

"He is," Marcie said. "He asked me if his dad was coming back as I was putting him bed. I told him that I hoped so, but all we could do is ask God to keep him safe and to watch over all of us. Then we prayed together and he fell asleep."

"I hope he shows up," Johnny said. "I can't imagine what it would be like to lose your father like that at that age. Did he say anything about his mother?"

"He said she was in heaven," Marcie said. "I think she died a few months ago."

"That's too bad," Johnny said. "I guess we are all he has right now. I hope to God we find his father tomorrow."

"I told him he could call me Aunt Marcie and you Uncle Johnny," Marcie said. "I hope that will give him the feeling of having some family until his dad gets back."

"That's good thinking," Johnny said. He felt tired again and let out a loud yawn as he stared silently at the fire.

"You sound tired," Marcie said. "I am a little worn out myself. It's been a long day."

"I want to thank you for all you've done and for your patience," Johnny said. "This trip hasn't started out like we planned."

"I had fun," Marcie said. "He's a real sweet boy."

"Yeah, he sure is," Johnny said. "You know, when I was checking into the deaths of that couple on Picacho Peak, I remember wondering what would have happened if they had a child. Would there be another orphan in the world?

"This was at the time I was questioning whether or not hiding out in the desert in a house made of straw was such a good idea. I was really missing my son Jerry and I wondered if I should try to adopt a son or something. You know, try to make the world a better place for someone else.

"The last month has been something else with all the death and destruction that came from me trying to protect that canal as a security guard. If I had stayed in that engineering job, all this stuff would have passed me by. I really thought I could retire from working and hide out in the desert. But now I realize that neither the desert nor retirement are places to hide from the world.

"Now I am starting to wonder why I came here so suddenly without waiting for my house to be finished. Have I switched from hiding from the world to running from it? If so, I think I am finding out that this is no place to run."

"You aren't running," Marcie said. "We came here to think about things and that's what you are doing. All these incidents are just strange coincidences of other people in trouble. Maybe the reason they find you is that you are a person that can help."

There was a long pause as they each stared into the bright orange flames of the fire. The flames wrapped themselves around the logs and rocks inside the fire ring.

"With the boy's mother gone, we are definitely in for the long haul on this one," Johnny said. "We have to find his father. I hate to think what is in store for him if we don't. I should have looked harder. I should have gone farther down the trail. The man is probably out there suffering because I didn't do enough."

"That's not true," Marcie said. "You kept your cool out there and made sure everyone was safe without going off half-cocked like some others would do. People need someone like you when they are in trouble. They need someone that can keep their cool under pressure and that cares about finding out the truth."

"I need you," she said. "Tommy needs you."

They both smiled and held hands as sparks from the fire flew high above their heads.

Chapter 8

Johnny Blue awoke to the sound of a bell ringing loudly above his head. He reached up from his prone position on the side couch in his trailer and turned off his alarm clock. It was six o'clock in the morning and the sun was just beginning to light up the window of his trailer. Marcie Foster looked down on Johnny from her perch on the bed above him. Tommy was still sleeping under the covers next to her.

"What are you doing?" Marcie whispered.

"I've got to go check on the status at the visitor center," he said. "Now that the sun is coming up, I think we need to start a search party if we can."

"You should have some breakfast first," Marcie said. She carefully swung her legs down over the side of the bed while Johnny opened a cupboard in the front of the trailer.

"I'll just grab a banana and a trail mix bar," he said. "It won't take long to go down there and find out what's going on and then take a better look at the trail."

"What do you want me to do with Tommy," she said. She nodded her head towards the boy who had kicked the covers off his legs and was snoring loudly.

"Let him sleep," Johnny whispered. "If he wakes up before I get back, just keep him occupied. I would not bring him down to the visitor center until you hear from me or the campground host. I'll hurry back if I find anything out."

Johnny leaned over the table below the bed and gave Marcie a peck on the cheek and thanked her for taking care of the boy. He exited the trailer with a banana, a trail mix bar and a squeeze bottle full of water in his hands.

As he drove through Loop-B he noticed a beige colored motor home parked in the campsite three spots down from his own. He had not noticed the vehicle when he had arrived at his site the night before and Marcie had not mentioned a new arrival. The new visitors must have arrived after he had gone to bed the night before. He wondered how they got past the washed out road at the park entrance. They must have already been in the park; but where?

He was too anxious to get to the visitor center and start looking for Tommy's father to give the new development any further thought. He made a note in his notebook to remind himself to check back with the new arrivals if he did not find Tommy's dad right away. He continued driving out of the campground.

By the time Johnny reached the visitor center, he had washed the banana and trail mix bar down his gullet with a quarter of the bottle of water. The orange sun peeked over the ridge on the eastern side of the canyon. Three wispy white clouds drifted through the light blue sky along the northern horizon.

Johnny parked his pickup next to a white camper van near the missing man's black pickup. A thin man with even thinner gray hair and dressed in blue denim overalls and a white long-sleeved shirt stood up off the bench near the visitor center. Johnny noticed the man was wearing white tennis shoes that looked out of place given his age and the rest of his outfit. The sides of the shoes appeared to be covered with fresh mud. He stretched his arms over his head and let out a loud long yawn.

Johnny greeted the man who subsequently introduced himself as Don Baumgardner. The two men shook hands.

"Any news about the missing man?" Johnny asked.

"Not a peep," Baumgardner said. "I relieved Ken at four o'clock and haven't heard anything but hoot owls and coyotes since."

"Any word on the ranger?" Johnny asked. He had driven by the ranger's residence on the way over and the area looked as deserted as it had the night before.

"Ken said that he hadn't seen hide nor hair of him since before the thunderstorm last night," Don said. "He figures he must have got caught outside of the park somehow and can't get past the hole in the road."

"How about you," Johnny said. "Are you in a hurry to get out of the park?"

"Nah, me and my wife Noreen are retired now," Baumgardner replied. "We aren't in a hurry to get anywhere."

"Got any idea what this missing guy looks like?" Johnny asked.

"No, why would I," Baumgardner replied.

"I thought maybe he set up camp or something and you may have seen him before he went hiking," Johnny said. He thought to himself that Baumgardner was being a little defensive and then he wondered if it was just himself being to suspicious.

"No, I don't recall seeing him in camp," Baumgardner said. "Noreen might have seen him when I was in the can or something. This his truck here?" He pulled out a package of cigarettes with a familiar green label and offered one to Johnny as he lit one for himself.

Johnny refused the cigarette. Baumgardner shaded his eyes with his hands and peered through the side window of the canopy of the black pickup.

"Don't look like they unpacked much at all," he said.

"I was hoping to do a better search of the trail," Johnny said. He pulled out his GPS unit and stared at the waypoints on the display screen. "I marked the spots where the boy lost his father with my GPS here and also with some small bits of paper."

"Seems like a lot of trouble to send those silver balls into outer space just so you can remember where you left something on the trail," Baumgardner said. "I'd rather trust my own sense of direction than some satellite out in space."

Johnny smiled. He knew the man was right. Modern technology had moved modern man out of touch with nature. People could no longer find their way without a map or a computer telling them where they were and where they were headed. Automobiles now came with talking computers and even devices that would take over the wheel and do the driving without any aid from the human driver.

"It's just a little hobby of mine," he said in response to Baumgardner's statement. "Keeps me out of trouble."

"Who is this boy you mentioned?" Baumgardner asked.

"Didn't Ken tell you that I found a boy who said his father was lost on the trail?" Johnny said.

"Didn't mention it," Baumgardner said. "Just said someone was lost out here and wanted me to sit here to see if he showed up."

Johnny made a mental note to ask Myerson who he had told about Tommy and to whom he had not mentioned the boy.

"I sure appreciate all your help," Johnny said. "It would be nice if we could get some support from the rangers."

"I wouldn't count on it," Baumgardner said. "We ought to do what we can for ourselves. People don't do that enough these days. They are always looking for someone to take care of them."

"I guess you are right," Johnny said. "I am going to head on down the trail to see what I can find. Care to join me?"

"No, I better wake up the missus and get breakfast started back at camp," he said. "Ken wanted me to let him know when you showed up so he could help with the search. I'll let him know you started down the trail."

Johnny shook Don's hand and noticed the van shaking as if someone was moving inside. He realized Don's wife must have been sleeping inside all the while they had been talking. He turned and walked towards the Oak Flat Trail trailhead. His GPS unit locked on and adjusted its display with his every move.

The morning air felt cool and moist on his face as he walked down the gentle slope of the trail. In contrast to Tucson's dry warm air, Johnny enjoyed the feeling of moisture on his skin. The sounds of the morning chatter of the local native birds filled his ears as he walked. From the nearby woods came the sound of a covey of mourning doves cooing in a solemn tone.

Johnny wondered what he would find on the trail in the daylight. It seemed there were only a few possibilities, either he would find Tommy's dad alive and in good health, alive and in not so good health, or he would not find him at all. Either way, he would have to decide on the appropriate action to take depending on what he found or did not find.

He looked ahead on the trail and saw a piece of white paper hanging on an oak tree branch. He looked at his GPS unit. The unit indicated that the first waypoint was farther down the trail. Johnny stopped on the path next to the piece of paper. It looked like the same piece he had left the night before and had the words "Last look" written on it, but it seemed to be in the wrong place. He remembered that the first mark on the trail was where Tommy had said he tripped over a tree root. There was no evidence of the root anywhere nearby. He remembered writing the words "Last seen" on the first marker. "Last look" should have been the third marker. Something was wrong. He had either walked right by the first two markers and his GPS waypoint was off, or the marker had been moved.

He continued down the trail. A second piece of paper appeared on an oak tree branch. The GPS unit indicated that he should not have even reached the first marker yet. The piece of paper had the words "Tommy waited" written on it. Johnny remembered those as the words he had written on the second marker. He looked around the quiet forest. Was he losing his mind as well as his GPS signal? He could not understand what was going on.

He looked closely at the ground around him. The dirt path was still moist from the rain and the overnight dew. He recognized a few tracks that matched the tread of his hiking boots and assumed that they had been put there the night before when he walked down the trail when he first arrived for his watch.

There were a couple of other tracks that looked flat with crosshatch lines. They looked like they could have been made by a flat bottomed tennis shoe or sandal. It was hard to tell but it looked like one of the tennis shoe tracks overlapped one of the hiking boot tracks. There were very few tracks at all because most of the trail was covered with rocks or other debris preventing any footprints from taking hold. He could not escape the feeling that something more was going on than just a simple case of a man lost in the woods.

He took his small digital camera out of his coat pocket. The camera was silver in color and no bigger than his GPS unit, about five inches long and two inches wide. He took several photographs of the footprints and returned the camera to his pocket.

He remembered that the second marker indicated where Tommy said he sat down on the trail and waited for his father, but that was on a short straight stretch between two curves in the trail. This marker was on a long straight stretch. Johnny felt confused and light-headed. He wondered if he had gotten enough sleep during the night. He decide would keep walking down the trail to the waypoints he had marked with his GPS unit

Farther down the trail he found the first waypoint he had marked the night before. A piece of paper hung from a nearby oak tree. Johnny read the writing on the paper; it read "Last seen." This matched what he remembered writing on the first marker the night before. He looked around and saw the root that Tommy had tripped over.

It was as if he had walked backwards along the trail coming to the last marker first and the first marker last. Was that possible, he thought. He shook his head and tried to regain his focus. Whether they had been moved or not was irrelevant, he needed to find Tommy's father. He was confident that he had come down the trail the same way he had the night before and his GPS unit confirmed that. He needed to continue down the trail and search for Tommy's father.

"Tom, are you there," Johnny yelled. He strained his ears listening for a response. There was none. The forest was silent except for the occasional chattering of birds and the rustling of oak trees in the wind.

He continued walking slowly down the trail looking carefully through the surrounding forest for any sign of Tommy's father while occasionally calling for him and listening for a response. He reached the second GPS waypoint. He recognized the area as the place Tommy had said he had sat and waited. He saw more of the hiking boot and tennis shoe prints on the flat straight stretch of the trail. He could not tell which had been put down first. He took more photographs of the footprints. He surveyed the area closely but saw no sign of the missing man.

He continued down the trail until he came to the third GPS waypoint. The ground was too hard to show any footprints. He looked around the area closely and saw no signs of the missing man. He yelled for him again and received only the sound of birds chattering as a response.

The air was cool under the shade of the oak trees. The dense forest still let in enough light for him to see the trail and the surrounding area. He felt confident that if the man were anywhere near this part of the trail he would see him. The underbrush was dense and thick. He wondered if Tommy's father could have rolled down the hill and still be lying under the bushes hidden from view unable to move or call out. He tried to put such disturbing thoughts out of his mind. He had to find the man alive and well for Tommy's sake.

He continued down the trail until he came to a wooden sign nailed halfway up the trunk of a small oak tree marking a fork in the trail. The words "River Access" were carved into the wood in weather-worn letters. The sign pointed to the right hand fork of the trail.

Johnny assumed that the left-hand fork was a continuation of the Oak Flat Trail and circled around to the visitor center and that the right-hand fork was the Gunnison Route he had read about on the park's web page the night before. He stood and listened intently. He thought he could hear the sound of the river water rushing by several hundred feet below him. He called for the missing man again and received no reply.

He stopped and examined the steep downgrade of the first several yards of the trail down to the river. The dirt path was embedded with loose rocks and twigs. A few feet down the trail, Johnny noticed several healthy green leaves scattered near the edge of the path. He recognized the leaves as coming from a serviceberry bush and noticed some purple berries on the ground next to them.

He had read about the serviceberry bush when he first discovered it on one of his previous trips to the canyon. He knew that the bush got its name when early settlers put flowers from the bush on graves after funeral services. He pushed the thought of funeral services out of his mind.

The leaves and berries looked out of place mixed with the dry oak leaves and small twigs on the trail. The leaves looked fresh and healthy. The nearest serviceberry bush was several feet away from the trail but close enough that its four foot tall branches could have reached the trail if bent down in the right direction.

"Halloo, anyone there," a deep voice broke through the silence of the forest interrupting Johnny's train of thought. He stood still and listened intently. The voice sounded as if it came from the part of Oak Flat Trail he had yet to travel.

Chapter 9

After Johnny had left the trailer to start his search for Tommy's father, Marcie got out of bed and started her morning routine. Camping out with no running water made her appreciate the comforts of home a little more. She filled the small stainless steel kitchen sink with water from the jugs she and Tommy had filled the night before and then washed her face and hands in the water and dried them with a dish towel. She glanced at the bed at the back of the trailer and saw that Tommy was still sound asleep. She caught a whiff of the remnants of the previous night's campfire as she put on her red jacket and stepped outside.

The morning air felt cool against her face. The chatter from the local birds began to diminish as the sun rose above the eastern horizon.

She walked towards the restroom and thought about Tommy. She enjoyed his company and could feel a sense of maternal instincts growing inside her. She had never had children. She had married in her early thirties and the restaurant kept her and her husband so busy, she guessed they never got around to having kids. She never had a strong desire in that direction, but spending the evening with Tommy stirred something inside her. She was just a few years past safe child bearing age, but maybe adopting a child could bring new meaning to her life; regardless of what happened with Tommy and his father.

She tried to think of what it would be like to have a child Tommy's age around; to get him ready for school every morning and take him to soccer practice in the afternoon; to read him bedtime stories and watch grow him up into a teenager and then a man.

There must be orphans his age out there in need of a good home. If she did take on the task, she would have to take it on in the interest of the child and not her own selfish motives. She would have to commit herself to making sure the child had everything he needed to come of age. Of course she knew it would not all be quiet nights in the forest. There would be struggles, but she believed that no problem was so complicated she couldn't learn to deal with it properly.

After leaving the pit toilet facilities she walked back to the trailer. A soft breeze rustled the trees as she walked down the dirt path to the asphalt road. She heard the trailer door open and quickened her pace back to camp. When she arrived she found Tommy sitting on the bottom step of the trailer with the door open. He was still wearing his pajamas. His hands were under his chin and his elbows on his knees as he stared down at the ground.

"Did you miss me, honey," Marcie said.

Tommy lifted up his head to see Marcie approaching from the camp road. He jumped off the step, ran towards her, wrapped his arms around her leg and buried his head in her waist.

"Oh, honey, I'm sorry," she said. "I just went to use the restroom. I didn't think you would get up so soon. I didn't mean to leave you alone."

Tommy looked up into her eyes and asked, "Did they find my dad?"

Ken Myerson walked towards Johnny on Oak Flat Trail. Myerson had traveled on foot from the South Rim Campground over the Uplands Trail. Between the two routes the men had taken, they had covered all of Oak Flat Trail except for the small leg between its intersection with Uplands Trail and the visitor center. The total distance covered between the two men was less than two miles.

"Any luck?" Myerson asked.

Johnny described his morning's walk and how it appeared that the pieces of paper he had used to mark the place he had found Tommy had been moved. He explained that he was in the process of examining the area around the "River Access" sign and that they were not far from the last place Tommy saw his dad.

"That's Gunnison Route," Myerson said pointing to the part of the trail past River Access sign. "I hear it is pretty steep, but I've never been down it myself. There is supposed to be an eighty foot chain about halfway down that will help you get over the real steep parts.

"I just came through Rim Rock and Uplands Trail and this part of the Oak Flat Trail. I looked pretty close at the woods and the trail and saw no evidence of the missing man. So I guess the only place left to look is down Gunnison Route."

"What about the ranger, any word from him?" Johnny asked.

"No word," Myerson said. "Louise, my wife, is going to drive the pickup around the park to see if she can find him, but I suspect he got caught on the other side of the washout. She's going to park over at the park entrance for a while to see if anyone shows up that can call for help. In the meantime, I figure we ought to do what we can."

"Do you want to search the Gunnison Route together?" Johnny asked.

"Seems like the thing to do," Myerson replied.

The two men started down the steep trail. Johnny pointed out the fresh leaves near the start of the path. They both bent down to examine the nearby serviceberry bush together. Some of the branches of the bush looked like they had been recently broken.

"Not sure what could have caused that," Myerson said. "Could have been an animal, I guess. I saw a few deer munching on serviceberry on my walk over here, but I doubt a deer would do that kind of damage; maybe a bear."

"Are there many bears in the park?" Johnny asked. "I've never seen one."

"There are a few, but they are real shy," Myerson said. "We are fortunate in that respect. This park has not had the trouble that Yellowstone and Yosemite have had over the years with all the tourists feeding bears and then being surprised when the bears rip apart their camps and automobiles to get at whatever food they have left. These thick woods are perfect for bears with all the acorns, berries, mice and ground squirrels they like to eat."

Johnny took several pictures with his digital camera and marked the location with a waypoint on his GPS unit. He had his doubts about a bear doing that much damage to the bush. If that was the way they treated the bushes that supplied them with berries for food, there would have been other bushes just as mangled. Was it possible that Tommy's father came upon a bear in the woods and been attacked? He pushed the thought from his mind. Surely, an attack by a bear would have caused a commotion that Tommy would have heard. The boy had not mentioned hearing any commotion on the trail, but then again Johnny had not specifically asked him about it. He made a note to talk to Tommy in more detail about what happened and then turned his attention back to finding the lost man and away from speculating on what might have happened.

The two men continued down the trail with Johnny in the lead. The path was steep and still a little wet from the rain the night before. The ground was firm underneath a layer of small gravel. There were few leaves or twigs down the middle of the path. The edges of the trail, however, were lined with debris as if it had been swept away from the middle towards the edge. Some of the pieces of gravel were sitting loosely on top of the trail and were covered with mud on top. Johnny took a picture of the trail. He was curious about why some of the gravel seemed to be recently disturbed and wanted to have a reference to study later.

A brown and white official Park Service sign marked the turn for the first switchback on the trail. The sign reiterated the fact that the trail led to the river and warned that a Back Country Access Permit was required to travel any farther on the trail.

"I don't suppose anyone will write us a ticket for not having a permit," Johnny said to Myerson.

"I suppose not," Myerson replied. His words came out in between deep breaths as he huffed and puffed from the exertion of controlling his speed on the steep downhill slope.

"Are you sure you are up to this?" Johnny asked.

"No problem," Myerson said. "I'm like an old vacuum cleaner. I may be noisy, but I can still suck in air with the best of them."

The two men continued their walk down the trail which switched back and forth as they moved farther down the steep canyon side. Johnny had to stop at each switchback corner to make a choice as to which way to go. It seemed that every corner was an opportunity for previous travelers to go off on a spur trail making the main trail hard to follow. After examining a few of the spur trails, however, he realized that they all looped back to the main trail and that as long as he stayed on the trail it would be hard to get completely lost.

The surrounding plant life began to change as they traveled deeper down the canyon. A slight breeze passed through the branches of tall fir trees whose trunks were covered with dark green moss. A half a dozen mourning doves burst into the air from an open area near the trail as the two men passed by. The weak cries of the birds were barely audible over the sound of their wings beating sharply against their breasts.

There was no sign of Tommy's father. The trail and surrounding brush seemed undisturbed. The brush had become less thick along the trail and there were open areas underneath the branches of the fir trees where Johnny could see down to the next level of switchback. As was common in such situations, previous hikers had taken it upon themselves to use the open areas as a shortcut to the next level of the trail rather than travel down to the end of the switchback. A few of the shortcuts looked as if they had been disturbed since the rain had fallen. Johnny took more pictures and continued down the trail.

The two men came upon a large fir tree growing up out of the center of the trail. The route broke into to paths around the massive tree. The path to the left went straight down ten feet to the next level of the trail and the effect of water and human erosion over the years was most evident on that side of the tree.

The path to the right circled around the tree lowering in one foot increments and forming a natural spiral staircase to the trail below. The roots of the tree had raised themselves above the ground at irregular intervals forming supports to keep the stair steps in place and reducing the effect of erosion from rain and hikers' boots.

When they reached the bottom of the natural staircase, the men came upon the chain mentioned in the description of the route to the river. Both men were breathing and perspiring heavily even though they had been traveling downhill. The steepness of the trail had caused them to exert considerable effort to keep from sliding down the mountain out of control. Johnny sat down on a small boulder next to the trail and tried to catch his breath. Myerson leaned against the trunk of a large fir tree in an effort to do the same. Johnny pulled out his squeeze bottle of water and offered it to Ken. Both men drank heartily between breaths.

Johnny stared at the one-inch thick chain tied around the trunk of a large fir tree at the top of the steep embankment below him. He noticed and oddly shaped pink-colored piece of paper lying at the base of the tree. He stared at the paper trying to figure out what it could be. Finally the image formed clearly in his mind of the wrapper for a popular brand of bubblegum neatly folded into the shape of a triangle. The mental exercise had taken his mind off his breathlessness and he could feel his breathing return to normal. He wiped the sweat from his forehead and took another drink of water from his squeeze bottle.

He got up and walked to the edge of the steep embankment and looked down. He was ready to suggest that they give up the search. It did not make any sense that Tommy's father would have come this far down the trail without his son at his side. Even if he had become disoriented, he would surely have noticed the change in the steepness of the trail and realized he was headed away from his son.

Johnny looked down the steep drop below his feet. He examined the chain tied around the trunk of the fir tree. The tree had tried to protect itself by enveloping the chain with a yellow sticky sap as it cut through its outer bark. Johnny could see that considerable damage had been done to the living organism. The chain hung above the rocky gully for thirty feet before touching ground and then disappearing behind a corner lined with tall green bushes. Johnny assumed the chain continued down the side of the canyon for another fifty feet as the park website had described.

He compared the chain to the cables on Picacho Peak used to aid hikers in their ascent and descent from that mystical mountain near his home in Arizona. The cables at the peak were more like hand rails for hikers to steady themselves. The chain in front of him provided more than just a hand rail. To descend the gulley in front of him, Johnny thought, he would have to repel himself down the embankment using the chain as his only means to keep from falling to a rocky death.

He surveyed the area where the chain disappeared around a corner. His eyes passed over the sharp rock and moist dirt carved out by the gulley. He stared closely at an odd shape partially covered by the leaves of a bush hanging over the gulley at the point where the chain disappeared. He called Ken Myerson over to verify what he thought he was looking at.

Myerson pushed himself away from the tree he had been leaning against and walked to the edge of the embankment near Johnny.

"What does that look like to you at the bottom of the chain?" Johnny asked.

"Looks like a tennis shoe to me," Myerson said. "And if I'm not mistaken, it looks like it is still filled with someone's foot."

"I hate to say it," Johnny said. "But I think we just found Tommy's father."

Chapter 10

After a brief discussion with Ken Myerson about what to do next, Johnny began the climb down the steep gully to the tennis shoe lying on the rocks thirty feet below him.

Before starting his descent, he took a picture of the view from above in case he disturbed anything on the way down. He grabbed onto the chain with both hands and slowly lowered himself backwards down the rocky cliff. He turned his head to the left to look for footholds as he moved down the gully.

Occasionally he glanced above him to see Ken Myerson watching his progress. They had decided that Ken would stay up above while Johnny determined whether there really was someone attached to the shoe and if so what condition that person was in. They had not decided what to do after Johnny made that determination.

The sound of rushing water grew louder as he moved down the cliff. When he came to a point a few feet above the curve in the embankment, Johnny paused and looked down below him. He could see a leg extending around the corner from the shoe. He felt nauseas and paused to take several deep breaths before continuing down the slope.

After a few minutes, he continued lowering himself down the gulley. He moved to the right side of the ditch to avoid disturbing any evidence and to stay clear of the body.

He lowered himself down even with the shoe and lifted his head to examine the rest of the scene. The body of a man in his late forties was lodged between to large sharp rocks jutting out of the side of the canyon wall. The man had on a long-sleeved red flannel shirt and blue denim jeans. The lower part of his jeans and the back of his white tennis shoes were streaked with mud.

Johnny lowered himself to another large rock sticking out of the ground and stood up straight. The skin on his palms was marked with deep red indentations when he released the chain from his grasp. He rubbed his hands together and then wiped them on his pants.

Johnny scrambled on his hands and knees across the gulley to where he could position himself above the man's body. He steadied himself with one hand by grabbing onto the branch of a serviceberry bush which hung over the side of the steep ditch. He pressed the fingers of his other hand against the side of the man's neck. There was no pulse. He noticed bruises on the side of man's neck and underneath his Adam's apple. He did not see any blood on the body or anywhere near it.

Johnny looked closely at the man's face. Something looked familiar about it. He continued to stare for a moment and then realized the man had the same facial structure as Tommy. The man was certainly Tommy's father.

He scrambled back to the chain on the other side of the gulley, looked up at Ken Myerson and shook his head in the negative. He tried to think of what to do next. He stood up and looked at the scene around him.

The bruises on the neck and lack of blood in the area made him suspicious. He pulled out his GPS unit and marked a waypoint. Then he took out his digital camera and took a picture of the man's body as it lay trapped between the boulders. He took more pictures of the surrounding area which consisted of the steep wall he had just climbed down, Douglas fir trees and various bushes along the gulley, and more of the same below him.

Under different circumstances, he would have enjoyed the natural wonders around him, but today his mind was clouded by the realization that a young boy had just lost his only parent.

He looked back up the cliff. A tall man wearing a dark brown pants and a light green shirt underneath a dark brown jacket appeared on the trail next to Ken at the top of the steep slope. The man wore a round wide brimmed hat on his head and a shiny gold badge on his jacket. The ranger had arrived.

Chapter 11

The ranger lowered himself down the steep embankment quickly as if he had done it a number of times before. He introduced himself as Ranger Harrison Dodge. He shook hands with Johnny and then moved over to the body and examined it for pulse and respiration.

"He's pretty cold," the ranger said. "He must have been dead for several hours."

"That's what I thought," Johnny said. "What'll we do now?"

"Well, I had to cross the washed out road on foot so I don't have any transportation or anyway to get a hold of anybody from here," the ranger said. "I think the first thing to do is to get the rescue people out here to take him away. I'll have to call in the State Police to collect photos and evidence of the scene, and then the Park Service will have to send out a special agent to investigate.

"Louise, Ken's wife can give me a ride back to the washout and then I can walk back to my truck and make the calls I need. I had to run into town last night and the road was gone when I got back. I didn't think there was any urgency to try to cross in the dark, so I stayed in town with a friend of mine. I guess that was the wrong thing to do. Damn it!"

He turned away from the body. Johnny also turned away and stared at the steep rocky cliff below him. As he had suspected, the chain continued on another fifty feet down the canyon. The gulley became less steep and finally ended beneath some tall fir trees next to several large boulders.

He wondered how long Tommy's father had been dead and if there was anything else he could have done the night before. If the man had simply fallen down the cliff and knocked himself unconscious, how long did he lay there alive while Johnny was searching for the ranger and eating dinner? Should he have gotten everyone together with lanterns and flashlights and searched in the dark after the storm had passed? Even if they had, what were the chances of even seeing the body at the bottom of the cliff in the dimly lit night? Surely, he would not have tried to lower himself down the chain in the dark.

He stared at the ranger who was also looking down the steep embankment. Johnny got the impression that the ranger was having similar thoughts about dereliction of duty. There was no time for second guessing. He turned his thoughts back to the immediate concern, the young boy who was now officially an orphan. He wanted to direct the ranger's thoughts in the same direction.

"There was nothing you could have done," Johnny said. "That thunderstorm raged on until almost dark. There was no way you would have found him down here."

"I guess you are right," the ranger said. "That's water under the bridge. We need to get him out of here before nightfall."

"I don't know if Louise told you, but we have his son in our trailer," Johnny said. "We found him on the trail just before the thunderstorm hit. He said he had lost his father. I guess that's the last time anyone saw him alive."

"He must have taken a wrong turn and fallen down the embankment," the ranger said.

"I guess so," Johnny said. "Something does not seem right though. The boy lost sight of him on Oak Flat Trail before they ever reached the River Access sign. Why would the guy turn onto this steep trail if his boy wasn't right by his side? Wouldn't he have waited for his son to catch up before left the main trail?"

"Maybe the boy was mistaken about where he saw him last," the ranger said. "How old is he?"

"He looks to be about five or six," Johnny said. "He seemed pretty accurate about where he lost his father. He showed me where he had tripped over a root on the trail and sat and waited for his dad to come back when he couldn't find him. That was a hundred feet or more before the River Access sign."

"Either way his dad is dead," the ranger said. "And I'm not equipped to do the investigation. We'll have to leave that up to the State Police and Park Police.

"I am also not equipped to take care of a little boy. Can you see to him while I try to get a rescue unit in here to take the body out and get the State Police to come in and do a crime scene investigation? The road will be out for at least a couple of days so we'll have to have a helicopter bring in the necessary people. It might be a day or so before we sort it all out. Right now you're all the boy has got."

Johnny felt a lump in his throat. "We'll see the boy through this," he said. The memory of the loss of his wife and child resurfaced and he quickly pushed it away. This was no time for self-pity or remorse for past opportunities lost. The present situation needed his full attention.

"What campsite are you in?" the ranger asked.

Johnny told him the site number.

"I'll come by your site later to talk to the boy and let you know what is going on," the ranger said. "You might want to hold off telling him about his father until I'm there. I've had some training in this area."

"Before I go, I better check for identification," he said. "We wouldn't want to assume we found the missing man and find out later he was somebody else."

He reached underneath the dead body and pulled out a black leather wallet. He opened it up and examined the man's driver's license.

"The picture matches the face," the ranger said. "Thomas Atkinson. That sound right?"

"The Thomas sounds right," Johnny said. "We never asked the boy his last name, but I can tell from the man's face that he has to be the boy's father or a close blood relative. The resemblance is uncanny."

Johnny took one last look around and then began the difficult climb back up the steep slope. He pulled himself up with the aid of the chain until he reached the top and Ken Myerson helped pull him up to the ledge. Johnny informed Myerson of what had transpired.

He took another long look down the steep slope. Something did not seem right. The man just would not have left his son alone to climb this far down the trail.

He shook hands with Myerson and slowly walked back up the path known as Gunnison Route. He wondered what he was going to say to Tommy when he got back to the campsite.

Chapter 12

When he pulled his pickup into the gravel parking spot next to his trailer, Johnny saw Tommy and Marcie sitting in the canvas-backed chairs next to the campfire ring. Marcie was pointing at a bird in a nearby tree and Tommy was following the direction of her arm with his eyes. Johnny got out of the pickup and walked towards them.

"How is everybody doing this morning," he said.

"All right," Marcie replied.

Tommy said he was doing fine.

"Did you find my dad?" he asked.

Johnny could feel his face turn red and a lump raise in his throat.

"The ranger showed up," he said. "He's out looking for him now. I thought I should make sure you are all right. I am sure your dad wants me to take good care of you until he gets back."

Johnny sat down on a log near the campfire ring, took a deep breath of the fresh mountain air and then expelled it with a heavy sigh. A blue jay let out a loud caw from a nearby thicket of scrub oak.

"We've been watching that bird fly around and yell at us for the last several minutes," Marcie said. "I think we might have invaded its territory and he is mad at us." She sensed that the news was not good from the search and tried to change the subject. She was not sure why Johnny was not being completely open about the situation, but she assumed he had a good reason.

"Maybe it has a nest around here," Tommy said.

"Like the one we saw in your book, right" Marcie said. They had spent the morning going over the boy's book on birds again.

"We could go on a walk around the campground and see if we can find one," Johnny said. "Would you like that Tommy?"

Tommy shrugged his shoulders and looked down at the fire grill. Johnny could tell his mind was preoccupied with thoughts of his father. He hoped he could find something to distract him with until the ranger came by to explain the situation.

His instinct told him he should sit down with the boy and explain what happened. He subscribed to the theory that bad news was best dealt with like taking off a bandage. It was better to just rip it off and get the pain over with and then let the healing begin. He decided instead to follow the advice of the ranger and let the bandage hide the wound for a little while longer.

"Why don't we go for a walk," Marcie said. She stood up and stretched her arms over her head. She knew Tommy was dying to find out about his dad and Johnny was not saying what he knew. She hoped a walk might break the tension and get Tommy's mind off the situation.

The air was warm and a slight breeze rustled the tall green grass intermixed with the serviceberry and sagebrush surrounding the campsite. Johnny stood up and stepped over next to Tommy's chair.

"How about a walk, Tommy," he said.

Tommy stood up and gathered his light jacket around him. His lips were closed tight and his eyes stared straight ahead. He had the look of a determined fighter focused on his opponent.

"What about my dad?" he asked. He looked straight at Johnny, but Johnny could not look him in the eye.

"Well the ranger is out on the trail right now and he is going to talk to us about your dad in a little while," Johnny said. "Do you know what a ranger is?"

"I know about Power Rangers," Tommy said. "They can help people when they are in trouble."

"This ranger can help people too," Johnny said. "He is like a policeman only he helps people in the woods."

Johnny took Tommy's hand and they started walking down the small dirt path that led to a dense forest of pine and oak trees. Marcie followed close behind.

"Let's keep an eye out for a bird's nest," she said.

Johnny felt Tommy's hand squeeze tighter as he looked up at the trees above them. A bird made a loud cawing sound from a short distance away.

"I think he is over there," Tommy said. He pointed to the inner circle of trees and bushes on the other side of the asphalt road several yards ahead of them.

They walked by a short tree stump and a small chipmunk scampered up the gray bark on the side, stood up on its haunches and rubbed its nose with its front legs. The three campers followed the trail to the black asphalt access road for campground Loop C.

A gray-colored female mule deer grazed silently on the tall green grass along the road. Johnny stopped and tightly squeezed Tommy's hand. Marcie stopped next to them and took the boy's empty hand in hers. All three closely watched the deer which was impervious to their gaze.

"Have you ever seen a deer before?" Johnny whispered to Tommy.

"I think so," Tommy whispered back. "Can I pet it?"

"I think it will try to run away if we get too close," Marcie said. "Maybe we should move on and let it eat."

Johnny pulled his camera out of his pocket.

"Do you want to take a picture of it," he said and let go of Tommy's hand.

Tommy nodded his head in the affirmative and Johnny showed him how to use the camera. After Tommy pushed the button, Johnny showed him the picture on the flat display on the back of the camera.

"Cool," Tommy said. He smiled as he stared intently at the small screen.

Johnny returned the camera to his pocket and both he and Marcie took Tommy by the hand and continued their walk. They quietly passed by the deer as it continued to graze without taking notice of them. As they walked around the loop, Johnny noticed the Baumgardner's white camper van parked in site C-twelve. The sites in Loop C had no electric hookups. They were generally used by tent campers, but some recreational vehicle campers used them when they did not feel the need for electricity. The van stood motionless in its gravel parking spot. Johnny assumed that the Baumgardners were either sleeping inside or off somewhere else in the park.

The sight of the van triggered the memory of the motor home he had seen in Loop B on his way to the visitor center in the morning. He reminded himself to check out the new arrivals when he returned to camp. He would ask Marcie what she knew about their neighbors once they were alone.

As they approached site C-one, the site nearest the loop entrance, Johnny noticed a yellow Volkswagen bug with a chrome-plated tailpipe sticking up into the air behind its rear mounted engine. A blue and gray nylon tent held up by black fiberglass rods was set up under small oak trees on a flat spot below where the vehicle was parked on the asphalt road. A small dark green camp stove with a dark green propane bottle sat next to a pink pack of bubble gum and a green flashlight on the picnic table next to the tent. A light breeze rustled the leaves on the oak trees surrounding the site. Several of the leaves fell onto the tent and slid down its side to the bare ground.

"Hey, how's the search going?" a voice from behind them asked.

They all three turned to see Luke Atkins walking towards them from the restrooms. Luke's young face looked tired. Johnny stared at it for a moment. Something about it seemed familiar. He drew his gaze away from the man's face and looked him up and down to try to get a feel for who he was and what he was doing camping alone in an out of the way national park.

Atkins was not wearing a shirt. His chest looked thin and pale; his abdomen taut. Johnny noticed two red abrasions on Luke's mid-section just above his denim pants. The red bandana on his head was a little off kilter and looked dirtier than when Johnny had observed him in the yellow light of the visitor center the night before.

"The ranger is out there looking now," Johnny said. "We are just going for a short walk on this nice morning."

He did not want to discuss the situation in front of Tommy, particularly from someone he hardly knew.

He introduced Marcie and Luke to each other and then suggested Marcie walk ahead with Johnny on the trail which cut a path through the woods surrounding the entrance to the campground loop.

With Tommy's hand still engaged with her own, Marcie walked towards the gravel path lined by tall green grass. She sensed Johnny's discomfort with Atkins and agreed with the idea of getting Tommy away from him. She noticed Atkins had a triangular shaped gold pin in his bandana. Something about it looked out of place.

"I would expect you to still be sleeping," Johnny said. "You had a late shift last night."

He looked at the dark bags under Luke's eyes and wondered if they were the result of lack of sleep or something else. He looked tired and listless.

"So the ranger finally showed up, huh?" Luke said. "Think he'll be able to find the guy?"

"We'll see?" Johnny said. "How about you, did you see any sign of him last night?"

"Didn't see nothing," Luke said. "It was pretty quiet out there."

"Did you go down the trail at all or just hang out at the center?" Johnny asked.

"You kidding?" Luke replied. "Walking from the campground in the dark without a flashlight was bad enough. I wasn't about to go down a trail that would take me to those cliffs above the river. That reminds me, I've got your flashlight here. Didn't even use it."

Atkins walked down to the picnic table and picked up the flashlight. He also grabbed the pack of bubblegum and stuck it in his pants pocket before Johnny got a chance to see what brand of gum it was. The flashlight had some gritty mud on its handle.

"What'd you do, lose your shirt in a poker game?" Johnny asked.

"It's just a little warm out today," Luke said. "Thought I might get some sun. I could use a little color on this body." He looked down at his white arms and chest.

"The ranger says it might be a couple of days before they fill that hole in enough to where we can get out of the park with our vehicles," Johnny said. "Hope you didn't have anywhere you needed to be over the next two days."

"I've got all summer to go nowhere if I want," Luke said. He leaned his back against the side of his Volkswagen.

"How do you like your VW?" Johnny asked. "Ever do any off-roading?"

"Not in this thing," Luke said. "I was lucky to make it up the hill to the park. I need to overhaul the engine when I get enough money."

"What are you going to major in at college?" Johnny asked.

"Just General Studies until I decide what I want to do," Luke said.

"Are your parents helping you out with the finances for that?" Johnny asked.

"My old man," Luke said. "He spends every dime he has on that witch he married after he divorced my mother twelve years ago. I'm going to have to get by on financial aid and any other handouts I can get.

"Care to make a donation to my college fund?"

"Not at this time," Johnny said. "Good luck to you though and thanks for helping out last night."

Johnny held out his hand and Luke shook it. He noticed several scratches on Luke's wrist which were not there when they had shook hands the night before. Johnny turned and walked down the trail to catch up with Marcie and Tommy.

They were waiting for him as he walked down the first hundred feet of the trail. The three companions continued their trip downhill past small pine and oak trees. Several species of birds kept up a cacophony of chattering and chirping as the hikers traveled through the forest.

The group followed the trail as it meandered along the rim of the canyon. At one point they stopped to gaze at the dark gray jagged cliffs on the north side of the chasm.

"How old are you, Tommy?" Johnny asked.

"I am five, no six," Tommy said. "Two days ago was my birthday and I had ice cream."

"Happy birthday," Johnny said. He wondered if the boy's story could get any more melodramatic, first losing his mother, then losing his father the day after his birthday. But, he knew from his own personal tragedies and experiences that tragedy seemed to come in bunches and that truth was sometimes stranger than fiction.

"You go to first grade next year don't you," Marcie said. "I could tell you are a good reader when you helped me read your book about birds."

"My dad bought me it for my birthday yesterday," Tommy said. "That was before he got lost. Do you think he will come back?"

Johnny squatted down so that he was at Tommy's level. He felt he could avoid the subject no longer.

"We don't know what will happen, Tommy," he said. "No one knows what is ahead of them in life. Sometimes good things happen and sometimes bad things happen. When something bad happens sometimes we feel scared or sad and that's okay. When we are sad we just need to remember that something good will happen soon and we will be happy again.

"Just remember that whatever happens, Aunt Marcie and I will be here to help you and make sure you are okay. You won't be alone, okay? Remember to always believe in yourself and your mom and dad no matter what happens. Don't lose faith that good things are going to happen."

Tommy nodded his head and Johnny hugged him tight. He breathed in sharply through his nose as he felt the tears welling up in his eyes.

"It does not look like we are going to find that bird's nest," Johnny said. "Let's head back to camp and see if the ranger has anything to say."

Chapter 13

When they arrived back at camp, Johnny had sent Tommy to the restroom by himself so he could talk to Marcie alone. He filled Marcie in on the details of finding the boy's father. She had suspected as much, and so was prepared for the news.

"Well we've got to make sure he gets through this all right," she said.

Johnny stared out into space as if deep in thought. He surveyed the campsite and the surrounding area and noticed the large motor home parked a few sites away; the one he had seen on his way to search for Tommy's dad a few hours earlier.

"Do you know anything about this motor home parked a few sites down?" Johnny asked.

"I noticed the vehicle parked there when I got up this morning," Marcie said. "But, I have not seen anyone around."

"Maybe I'll pay a welcoming visit to our new neighbors," Johnny said.

"What are you up to?" Marcie asked.

"I don't know," Johnny said. "The situation on the trail did not seem right and these people weren't here last night. I am curious as to where they were when Tommy and his dad were out on the trail and where they were afterwards."

"Just be careful," Marcie said.

Tommy arrived back in camp from the restroom.

"Why don't you two start the fire and get out some hot dogs," Johnny said. "How does hot dogs roasted over a fire sound for lunch?"

"Good," Tommy said as he wiped his hands on his shirt.

Johnny walked out of the camp towards the motor home. He tried to prepare himself for whatever he would find in the campsite of the new arrivals. He knew he needed to keep an open mind and accept everything at face value if at all possible. He needed to keep his suspicious nature under control for the sake of his own sanity and for the sake of Tommy's future.

As he approached the site he noticed the clip on the post with the site's number was empty. The rules required that the top part of the payment envelope be filled out and attached to the post. Johnny pushed the thought out of his mind and tried to assume a positive attitude towards the strangers he was about to meet.

"Hello, anyone around," he said loudly as he approached the beige colored behemoth parked in the site.

"Over here," a male voice responded from the other side of the large vehicle.

Johnny walked around the front of the motor home to find a gray haired man and blonde woman sitting on two padded lounge chairs underneath an awning attached to the home. The man had on a pair of colorful shorts and flat-bottomed leather sandals. His chest was tan and covered with silver colored hair. The woman had on a colorful one-piece bathing suit, white sandals, sunglasses and a wide brimmed straw hat with a silk sash that matched her bathing suit. Her arms and legs were tan and her bosom ample. She stared out into the distance without taking notice of Johnny. Two large glasses of iced tea each with a slice of lemon and a straw sat on a small plastic table between the two chairs.

"What can I do for you?" the man said without getting up.

Johnny introduced himself and said he was just stopping by to say hello. He had not seen them come in before the thunderstorm and wondered how they got past the washed out road.

"What washed out road?" the man asked. He had introduced himself as Jay Fielder and the woman as his wife as Noreen with the same last name.

"The road into the park," Johnny said. "Didn't you come in after the thunderstorm yesterday afternoon?"

"No, we were at the end of the road on that nature trail," Fielder said. "We had to run back to the motor home just as the storm reached us. We waited out there for it to pass and watched the sun go down and then I guess we lost track of time playing cards and didn't get to our campsite until late.

"You say the exit to the park is washed out?"

Johnny described how he had found the road the night before while the storm was still raging.

"The ranger said it will be a couple of days before the road is repaired," Johnny said. "Are you in any hurry to go anywhere?"

"Not us," Fielder said. "We haven't got a care in the world and no place to be. I played that dot-com boom just right didn't I, honey?"

His wife stared out into the distance without acknowledging the question. Johnny noticed that Mr. Fielder was softly chewing gum as he spoke.

"Have you been out on the Oak Flat Trail at all?" Johnny asked. He had purposely not mentioned the situation with Tommy and his father. He thought it was better to let the ranger advise the campground occupants of the tragedy if he felt it necessary.

"Which trail is that?" Fielder asked.

Johnny described the location of the trail near the visitor center.

"We went down to that overlook below the center, if that's what you mean?" Fielder replied.

Johnny tried again to describe the location of the trail near the overlook.

"I guess not," Fielder said. "Look we're trying to get a little relaxation in so maybe we'll see you around."

Johnny turned and walked out of the campsite back towards his own. On his way back, he thought about what he had learned from the Fielders. They seemed preoccupied with relaxing by themselves and not much interested in other people. Mr. Fielder was chewing gum which could match the pink bubblegum wrapper at the top of the gulley. He had flat bottom sandals that could match the shoe prints Johnny had seen on the trail. He caught himself getting carried away again. The couple were obviously too preoccupied with themselves to be involved with anything nefarious, if there was even anything nefarious to be involved in.

Johnny silently reprimanded himself and turned his thoughts to Tommy as he walked back to camp. He joined Marcie and their young charge around the small campfire in the warm late morning sun. He picked up a stick with a hot dog on the end off of the picnic table and joined Marcie and Tommy in roasting the sausage over the fire.

"Just make sure you don't let it fall in the fire," Johnny said to Tommy. "Have you ever cooked hot dogs over a fire before?"

"I don't think so," Tommy said. "One time we roasted marshmallows though."

"That's fun too," Johnny said. "Maybe we can roast some marshmallows tonight."

"I brought some graham crackers and chocolate so we can have s'mores," Marcie said. "Have you ever had s'mores, Tommy?"

"I don't think so," the boy replied. "What are s'mores?"

"You roast a marshmallow and put it on top of a piece of chocolate on a graham cracker," Marcie said. "How does that sound?"

"Good," Tommy replied. He noticed that the end of his stick had caught on fire and jerked it back away from the flames. He held the stick in front of his face and blew on it until the flames went out.

"Hey, Tommy," Johnny said. "Do you know why they call them s'mores?"

Tommy answered, no.

"Because if you ever eat one you always say, can I have s'more," Johnny said. "Do you get it?"

Tommy rolled his eyes and smiled.

"Why don't you let me help you fix your hot dog?" Marcie said to Tommy. "It looks like that one is done."

She helped him remove the charred piece of meat from the stick and set it on a paper plate on the picnic table. She fixed a hot dog bun with mayonnaise, the way Tommy said he liked it, then she put the hot dog on the bun, set it down on a paper plate and added a handful of potato chips. Tommy sat down on the picnic table bench in front of the plate and Marcie set a can of orange soda down in front of him. The boy bit ravenously into the hot dog and took a drink of soda. He swung his legs back and forth underneath the picnic table bench.

Johnny moved to the other side of the picnic table and sat down next to Marcie. The two quickly fixed their individual lunches and began to eat.

"How's that hot dog, Tommy?" Johnny asked.

"Good," he said.

"These are good," Marcie said. "There's nothing like cooking your own food for yourself in the great outdoors." She felt better about the situation. Being a restaurant worker, she knew that food usually picked up a person's spirits. Tommy's mind seemed to be at rest as he ate.

"I take it you don't miss the restaurant right now, do you?" Johnny asked.

"The furthest thing from my mind," Marcie said.

She had not thought about it, but it was true she did not miss it. She had given her two employees the week off while she took her trip and put up the closed sign for the first time since she had started the business with her husband. She had left her day-to-day worries behind and it felt good.

A chipmunk climbed up onto the end of the picnic table. The rodent was golden brown with two black stripes running down its back. It sat on its haunches and rubbed its nose.

"I guess we aren't the only ones that are hungry," Johnny said.

He was having a little trouble swallowing his food. The image of the dead man's bruised neck kept popping into his mind. He wondered if he did the right thing by taking the ranger's advice and not telling Tommy himself. He had been tense around Tommy and Marcie all day and he was sure they both sensed his preoccupation.

"Can I feed him," Tommy asked. He pointed to the chipmunk which was now waving its two front legs towards Tommy from its perch at the end of the table.

"That's not a good idea," Johnny said. "If we feed wild animals they get used to having food given to them and then they won't know where to get food after we leave."

"Better to let the wild ones grow wild," Marcie said.

Tommy washed the last remnants of his hot dog down with a gulp from his can of orange soda and then continued eating the potato chips on his plate.

"Halloo," a voice said loudly from the edge of the campsite. "Mind if I approach?"

Ranger Harrison Dodge appeared on the path on the edge of the woods surrounding the campsite.

"Come on over," Johnny said. "We are just finishing up lunch. We can offer you some potato chips and soda if you are hungry. If you want a hot dog, you'll have to cook it over the fire yourself."

"I could use a soda," the ranger said. "Maybe we can all sit around the fire here. I have some information I need to go over with you."

"Have a seat," Marcie said. She got up and handed the ranger a wet can of soda from the cooler.

"I am Marcie and this is Tommy and I believe you've met Johnny," she said. All three proceeded to the chairs and logs surrounding the campfire. The ranger shook the hand of each camper and greeted them individually with a warm, but tired smile.

"Why don't you sit next to me on the log here," the ranger said to Tommy. "I'd like to talk to you."

"Did you find my dad?" Tommy asked as he sat down next to the ranger.

"That's what I want to talk to you about," the ranger said. "Before I begin, can you tell me what your last name is?"

"Atkinson," Tommy said. "I'm Tommy Atkinson and my dad is Tom Atkinson. Did you find him?"

The ranger sat down next to Tommy and put his arm around his shoulders. Marcie and Johnny sat on the canvas-backed chairs nearby listening intently but trying not to seem to anxious so as not to add any stress on the boy.

"Do you know what happens when people die, Tommy" the ranger said solemnly.

"My dad said that when my mom died she went up to heaven and someday we will all die and be in heaven together," Tommy said. "Did my dad die?"

"I am afraid so," the ranger said.

Tears welled up in Johnny's eyes and Marcie blew her nose on a tissue.

"How did he die?" Tommy asked. He wiped his eyes with his hand and sniffled with his nose.

"I think he fell down and hit his head on some rocks," the ranger said. He was impressed with the way the boy was taking the news, but he knew he would need some time to work through the information. "I don't think he suffered. I think he went to heaven real fast."

Tommy's eyes began to swell with tears. He stared out into the forest as if in a trance. A Peregrine falcon flew overhead and let out a loud screech.

"Did anyone else come to the park with you?" the ranger asked.

"No," Tommy sniffled. "Me and my dad drove over some big mountains to get here by ourselves."

"Do you have a mom or any brothers or sisters?" the ranger asked. "Or anybody that can take care of you?"

"No," Tommy said. "Me and my dad were living by ourselves after my mom got sick and was in the hospital." Tears rolled effortlessly down his soft cheeks as he spoke.

"Do you ever go visit your grandma or grandpa?" the ranger asked.

"I had one grandma but she went to heaven to," Tommy said. He sniffled again.

"Okay how about aunts or uncles?" the ranger asked.

Tommy answered in the negative.

"Who takes care of you when your dad is at work?" the ranger asked.

"My mom used to and then she got sick and my dad stopped working," Tommy said. "Sometimes he would leave me at Clarissa's house and I would play with Chris."

"Was Clarissa your babysitter?" the ranger asked.

Tommy answered yes.

"Do you know her last name?" the ranger continued the interrogation.

Tommy answered in the negative.

"Do you know what city you live in," the ranger asked. He pulled a small notebook and a pen out of the breast pocket of his jacket.

"Tucson, Arizona," Tommy said. "My dad made me memorize my address in case I got lost."

He recited the numbers of the address which was on Ina Road. Johnny and Marcie looked at each other through tearful eyes and wondered at the coincidence that the boy should live within a half hour drive of her restaurant and Johnny's ranch.

"Aren't you something," the ranger said. "You remember all those numbers by heart. That's real good."

Marcie and Johnny both smiled admiringly at the boy and laughed through their tears.

"It's going to take a few days before we can leave the park and find someone to take care of you," the ranger said. "How would you feel about staying with Marcie and Johnny here?"

"Okay," Tommy said. "Can I go home with them?" He wiped the tears from his eyes with his sleeve.

"We'll have to see," the ranger said. "Do you like Johnny and Marcie?"

Tommy nodded his head.

Johnny got up, walked over to Tommy and bent down in front of him.

"You know we will always be here to help you Tommy, so I don't want you to worry," Johnny said with tears in his eyes.

Tommy jumped off the log, threw his arms around Johnny's neck and started sobbing. Marcie rubbed his head with her hand and tried to comfort the boy.

"Everything is going to be all right," she said. "We are going to take good care of you."

The sound of a helicopter approaching in the distance broke the silence of the forest.

"That must be the rescue crew," the ranger said. "I have to go. I'll check in with you folks later."

Johnny felt a cool breeze blow through his shirt as he stood up with Tommy's arms still wrapped around his neck. He thought he heard the sound of thunder in the distance and looked towards the east.

He could see large black clouds slowly making their way towards the canyon as he carried Johnny to the trailer to put him to bed.

Chapter 14

Johnny laid Tommy down on the bed in the trailer as Marcie came inside and shut the door behind her. Her eyes were red and she made a sniffling sound with her nose. Tommy was still sobbing as he stretched out on the bed.

"Will you be okay watching him?" Johnny asked. "I'd like to go see if I can help with the rescue."

"Take your jacket," Marcie said. "It looks like another thunderstorm is on the way."

Johnny grabbed his light jacket off the couch, started towards the door and then stopped and turned back. He tried to think of where he was most needed. Should he stay with the boy or act as his representative in the handling of his father's remains.

"I'm sure he'll be all right," Marcie said. "He just needs to have a good cry."

"I'll leave the truck here and hike down the trail," Johnny said to Marcie. "If you need anything, don't hesitate to drive down to the visitor center and get me."

He wrapped his arms around her and held her for a moment. "Sometime in the future we are going to get to spend a relaxing day together," he said.

"Tommy and I will find something to do without you," Marcie said. "Won't we, Tommy."

Tommy nodded his head. He was sitting up with his feet dangling over the edge of the bed and rubbing his eyes with his hands.

"Maybe you can look for some more of those birds from your book," Johnny said to Tommy. "Don't worry son, we're here for you."

Johnny walked out of the trailer into the cool afternoon air. The wind blew small leaves around the campsite as he walked towards the dirt path that led through the woods. He glanced back towards the Loop B access road and noticed that the Fielder's motor home was no longer parked in their campsite.

He walked through the woods to the access road for campground Loop C. As he walked down the asphalt road, he recognized the white camper van parked in spot C-twelve as belonging to Don Baumgardner, the man he had relieved from his post at the visitor center.

The van jostled slightly as if someone was moving inside. Johnny glanced at the side window of the vehicle and thought he saw two wrinkled hands opening the lid of a black metal box. The box looked similar in shape and size to the lock-box Johnny had seen in the back of the dead man's pickup the night before. The shades on the van window were pulled down to within a few inches of the bottom, preventing him from seeing who belonged to the hands on the box. The hands were small and wrinkled with blue varicose veins. Johnny reprimanded himself for looking into other people's windows and continued walking down the road but made a mental note to check to see if the black lock box was still in the back of the Tommy's father's pickup.

From a distance of a hundred feet or so, he could see Luke Atkins' yellow Volkswagen bug parked outside his campsite. As he approached the site, Johnny could see Luke Atkins lying on his back on top of the picnic table. A triangular-shaped gold pin on Luke's red bandanna sparkled in the sunlight from its perch on top of his head. The young man's right hand lay across his forehead and his left leg was bent so that his knee stuck up in the air.

Johnny walked by the campsite without disturbing the resident. He turned down the dirt path known as Rim Rock Trail. He followed the path downhill for a few hundred yards through the woods until he came to the turnoff for the Uplands Trail. He could see black clouds on the eastern horizon moving quickly towards the canyon as he turned left on the trail which he knew would eventually lead to the Oak Flat Trail and the visitor center.

He thought about what to do with Tommy. He vowed not to leave him alone until he knew his exact fate. If what Tommy had said was true, he was a true orphan with no one to take care of him. A paternal instinct grew inside Johnny's heart. He tried to imagine what it would be like to adopt the boy and raise him on his own.

He was sure most people would say that raising a child in the middle of the desert with no other kids around was not the ideal situation and he understood the point. Children needed playmates and play time everyday. He was sure he could provide for some of the boy's needs; perhaps buy a few horses or cattle and get him involved in raising them. Still the boy needed to be around kids his own age. He would get some of that at school and he could sign up for extracurricular activities like soccer or little league baseball.

What were the other alternatives, he thought. Make him a ward of the state? Put him in a foster home on the off chance someone might adopt him? The boy had some real hard luck and whether he was legally or morally obligated to or not, Johnny was determined to make sure he had everything he needed to overcome his present troubles.

He came to the point where the Uplands Trail crossed the park access road. He crossed the road and returned to the trail which now traveled through a grassy meadow lined by small oak trees. Three large female mule deer grazed silently on the grass. They took no notice of Johnny as he passed by them.

Johnny stopped and stared at the graceful animals. He noticed a large buck at the edge of the surrounding forest on the other side of the female deer. With its black eyes, the buck stared intently in Johnny's direction. Its large hollow ears pricked up in the air next to its four point antlers. He wondered if the buck sprung to attention because of his concern for his mate or over concern for his own safety based on past experiences at losing family members at the hands of a hunter or was he just curious and suspicious of everything out of the ordinary.

Johnny continued down the trail into the woods. The path was dark and shaded from the sunlight by the surrounding closely spaced oak trees. He thought about Marcie. He had not had much of a chance to talk with her since the long drive from Tucson. He felt like they had gotten to know each other pretty well on the drive. There were no great surprises. They had known each other for a few months before they began the trip and they each knew that the other was a decent person. They each knew that the other had suffered a tragedy in their lives from which they were not fully healed. They knew they were both people that were not necessarily looking for more out of life, but just trying to live their lives the best they could with the hands they were dealt.

He felt compelled to closely observe the trail as he walked. The path was made of hard dirt covered with leaves and twigs. He noticed a pink piece of paper underneath the debris and bent down to examine it. It was another bubblegum wrapper shaped in the form of a triangle. He felt his imagination running away with him again and tried to stop it. He left the wrapper where it lay on the off chance that the investigators might see it as evidence in a crime. His thoughts turned away from the immediate situation and back to his own life.

He tried to imagine what life would be like if Marcie and he were together. Would they each want to continue on the paths they had started down, she with her restaurant and he with his straw-bale retreat in the desert? Or would they want to start over as a team working towards the same purpose in life? For what purpose, he did not know.

That was one of the objectives of the trip to Black Canyon; to re-evaluate the direction his life was headed. Did he really want to live as a recluse in the desert or was it time to start living that age-old fantasy of traveling the world.

He was financially secure as long as he managed his money wisely, so his options were wide open. He had always found that it was easier to make decisions when he was backed into a corner with limited options. He felt a little uncomfortable trying to decide how to proceed when too many options were available. He liked to think of himself as a vagabond letting the wind direct him towards his next destiny.

He came to the point where the Uplands Trail crossed the park access road again. Dark drops of rain spotted the gray asphalt as Johnny crossed the road into the oak forest on the other side. He could hear the sound of helicopter blades beating against the air. He looked up to see a bright yellow flying machine cruise by overhead.

The wind picked up as he continued down the Uplands Trail to where it intersected with the Oak Flat Trail. He turned to his left on the new trail and continued walking downhill. He thought to himself that Ken Myerson must have traveled the same route earlier in the morning and Luke Atkins must have traveled the same route by moonlight the night before.

The rain and wind picked up. The dark clouds had reached the north rim of the canyon and continued their path towards the south rim. Johnny reached the turnoff to Gunnison Route which led to the embankment where Tommy's father's body lay wedged between two boulders half way down. He could hear voices shouting over the sound of the helicopter blades beating against the wind.

He reached the top of the embankment in time to see a shiny metal stretcher containing the body of Tommy's father being loaded into the helicopter hovering above the canyon.

"That's that," Ken Myerson said as he turned to acknowledge Johnny's presence. The campground host stood at the edge of the embankment looking at the helicopter hovering above the canyon.

Johnny looked down from the top of the embankment to see Ranger Harrison Dodge signaling for the helicopter to leave. A loud clap of thunder pierced the air as the helicopter dipped to one side and flew away.

Chapter 15

The ranger used the eighty foot long chain attached to the tall fir tree to pull himself up to the top of the embankment where Johnny Blue and Ken Myerson waited for him. Johnny and Myerson each grabbed an arm and helped pull the ranger up to the ledge. The ranger brushed the dirt from his pants and tried to catch his breath form the climb.

"They'll be taking him to the morgue in Montrose for a post-mortem examination," he said in between huffs and puffs.

"What about the State Police and Park Police investigators?" Johnny asked. "Didn't they come on the chopper?"

"The State Police came in and collected evidence around the scene," the ranger said. "They took some pictures and bagged the guy's hands and will turn it over to the Park Service. A special agent from the law enforcement division of the Service will be out tomorrow."

Johnny paused and looked down the embankment where the body had been trapped between two rocks just a few minutes earlier. The area looked vacant; as if nothing out of the ordinary had happened.

"What evidence did they collect?" Johnny asked.

"Just some of the debris around the body," the ranger said. "They looked around up here and found a bubblegum wrapper and took that. I don't know, it looks to me like the guy got ahead of his son on the trail, may have got a little disoriented or whatever and then fell down the cliff."

"I took some photographs of the scene with my digital camera and could put them on a CD if you think the investigators might be interested," Johnny said.

"I am sure they'll take anything they can get," the ranger said.

"Did they say anything about the bruises on the man's neck and the fact that there was no blood even though it looked like he hit his head pretty hard?" Johnny asked. The wind from the approaching storm began to blow through the trees and he had to speak loudly over the sound of the rustling branches and gusting winds.

"They really weren't looking that close," the ranger said. "The medical examiner will have to look at the bruises and determine the cause of death. They had very little time to work with and the Park Police investigator that comes in tomorrow will do a more detailed investigation."

"Did they look at anything farther up the trail?" Johnny asked. "Ken and I saw some bushes that seemed pretty broken up."

"What do you think, Ken?" the ranger asked. "Did you see any evidence of anything but a fall?"

"I don't know," Ken said. "The bushes did look a little torn up, but I can't say what could have caused the damage. Best to let the investigators investigate."

"How about the other campers? Do any of them know anything about this guy?" the ranger asked.

"I asked each one when I got them to stand watch," Myerson said. "None of them had even seen the man or his pickup.

"Come to think of it though, that young kid with the bandanna acted a little strange when I relieved him last night. I got here a little early and he was coming off the trail. He was wiping his hands pretty good on his jeans and seemed kind of nervous. He was sucking in wind pretty hard; almost swallowed his gum. "

"The boy told me he didn't go down the trail at all on his watch," Johnny said. "I still stand by my claim that the markers I had laid down the previous evening had been moved somehow. Whether he moved them or someone else did, I'd like to find out what happened."

"All right I'll have a little chat with him when I get back to camp," the ranger said. "I really think we need to leave the investigation to the professionals. They won't appreciate anyone contaminating evidence whether their intentions are good or not."

A strong wind rustled the leaves under their feet. A flash of lightning lit up the eastern sky and a few seconds later a clap of thunder rattled the woods.

"Looks like we are in for another storm," Myerson said. "We better head on back."

"Anyone bring a vehicle?" the ranger asked.

The other two men shook their head in the negative.

"Might as well walk back together," the ranger said. "The Uplands Trail ought to be the quickest."

The three men started walking up the steep dirt path towards the intersection of Gunnison Route and Oak Flat Trail with the ranger in the lead followed by Myerson and then Johnny.

Johnny thought about what the ranger had said. He seemed convinced that the death was an accident, but a lot of things did not add up. It was not the ranger's fault. Johnny was sure he had not signed up for the job to investigate homicides or accidental deaths. That's why the Park Service had its own investigation unit. He remembered reading about how short-handed and unprepared rangers were to enforce laws in the national parks and monuments.

The problem was at a crisis level in Johnny's home state of Arizona. A ranger had been killed in Organ Pipe National Monument when he tried to stop gunmen from a drug cartel from crossing from Mexico to the United States through the monument. Every day hundreds of illegal aliens and drug smugglers crossed through the monument with only a few rangers to try to stop them. Many of the rangers did not consider that task part of their job description and felt like they were ill-equipped and inadequately trained to perform it at any rate.

Organ Pipe was at the extreme end of the spectrum as far as dealing with illegal activity, but Johnny could empathize with Ranger Harrison. He was sure he had his hands full trying to protect the park from and for its visitors. The hole in the road at the entrance to the park was going to make his job that much harder over the next several days. The last thing he needed was to spend time investigating a death in the park.

Johnny turned his thoughts back to Luke Atkins. He suspected that the young man had been on the trail the night before and lied about it to him. There could be a simple explanation, if so Johnny would like to hear it. Maybe he just stepped into the woods to relieve himself and choked on his bubblegum so he was breathing hard when Myerson saw him. Or maybe he was curious and went down the trail to get a look at the scene of the incident and didn't want to admit it in case he contaminated any evidence.

Johnny wondered if he was letting his imagination get the best of him. He had doubted his instincts when he had found that couple dead on Picacho Peak a couple of weeks earlier, but in the end his instincts had been right and he had solved a murder case. As much as he liked to be right, he hoped he was not heading down the same path. He hoped that the death of Tommy's father was just another case of an accidental death in the woods.

As they approached the part of the path where Gunnison Route intersected with Oak Flat Trail, Johnny looked at the area off to the right where he and Myerson had found a serviceberry bush with broken branches. He saw a glint of metal lying in the soft dirt underneath the bush and left the trail to pick it up. The other two men stopped near the "River Access" sign on Oak Flat Trail and turned to watch Johnny's activities.

"Looks like some kind of gold pin," Johnny said. "It says *Don't Mess with Texas* and it is in the shape of that state."

"More evidence?" the ranger said as Johnny walked towards him from the trail below. He made the sign for imaginary quotation marks with his fingers in the air when he said the word "evidence."

"You tell me," Johnny said. "Ken and I noticed the bush had been disturbed recently before we found the body. It might be important to the investigators." He pulled out his camera and took a picture of the pin.

"All right, I'll make sure they know about it," the ranger said. He pulled out a small notepad and a pen. He wrote down something on the pad and then asked Johnny for the pin. The ranger stuck the gold trinket through the page on which he had written a description of it.

"I think I'll take Rim Rock Trail back," Johnny said. "I'd like to take some pictures of where I left those pieces of paper."

"Suit yourself," the ranger said. "Ken and I will go back on Uplands; it will be quicker."

"Stop by my place when you get back to camp so I know you are all right," Myerson said.

Myerson and the ranger started walking up the right hand side of Oak Flat Trail towards Uplands Trail. Johnny started to the left towards Rim Rock trail and the visitor center. The wind rustled the trees along the trail and a clap of thunder sounded in the distance. Johnny passed by the paper markers he had left and verified that they were still in the same locations that he had last seen them in. He took pictures of each one, unsure of what value they might have.

As he approached the visitor center, Johnny surveyed the area closely. The parking lot was empty except for the dead man's black pickup truck. He walked to the back of the pickup and peered through the glass door on the canopy.

He felt uneasy about performing his next actions. He wished he would have brought the subject up with the ranger, but he did not want to come off sounding like some paranoid kook. The ranger seemed preoccupied with his normal duties in the park and not concerned about investigating any possible crimes.

Johnny swiveled his head around to ensure that no one was watching. He slowly twisted the handle on the door to the truck's canopy and lifted it up until it latched over his head. He took one more look around and climbed inside. He pulled his notepad out of his jacket pocket and turned to the page where he had made notes about the contents of the pickup when he first climbed inside to find some clothes for Tommy.

He had drawn a small diagram of the pickup bed and square boxes for each item. He went down the list, the cooler was in its place, next to it sat the two sleeping bags, next to the sleeping bags the lid on the cardboard box marked "camping supplies" was open.

Johnny tried to remember if the box was open the night before. He did not think it was and had not noted the fact on his pad. The next item on the diagram was the black metal lock-box. Johnny looked at the vacant space between the cardboard box and the large blue bag; the lock-box was gone.

As young people do, Tommy began to recover quickly. Soon after Johnny had left him and Marcie alone in the trailer, he was up and around and curious about the world. Marcie helped him wash his face and gave him a soda to drink and the boy started to feel better. They sat at the table in the trailer and began flipping through the pages of Tommy's book on birds.

"Tell me about your friend Chris that you visit at Clarissa's house," Marcie said. She had remembered Tommy mentioning the names when the ranger questioned him about relatives. "Is he the same age as you?"

"Yes," Tommy said. "His mom has horses and one time she let me ride one."

"Did you like that?" Marcie asked.

"It was fun," Tommy said.

"Does he like trains as much as you?" Marcie asked. Earlier she had learned of Tommy's fascination with locomotives and discovered that he had several books on trains back home.

"He has his own train set," Tommy said. "It has tracks that go in a circle and it runs on batteries and flashes lights and makes a train sound when it runs."

Marcie could tell the boy was excited about the subject and was glad to see him distracted from the situation with his father.

"What else do you do when you stay at Chris's?" Marcie asked.

"Play soccer and basketball," Tommy said. "And chutes and ladders."

"I like chutes and ladders," Marcie said. "I wish we had that game here, we could play. Did you know that Uncle Johnny and I live near Tucson where you and your dad lived?"

Tommy's eyes lit up and he stretched his neck as he raised his head in interest. He shook his head no in answer to Marcie's question.

"Well we do," Marcie said. "I have a restaurant and Uncle Johnny lives on a ranch in the desert."

"Does he have horses?" Tommy asked.

"Not right now," Marcie said. "But someday, maybe. Would you like to come visit us in Tucson?"

"Can I live with you?" Johnny asked.

Marcie smiled and brushed his hair back with her hands. She had a feeling this question was coming and was not sure of how to answer. It was a complicated situation. The government would have to be involved and who knew if someone else would come along to lay claim to the child.

"We'll have to see," Marcie said. "Some people will come by to ask you what you want to do, so you will have to tell them. Whatever you decide, Uncle Johnny and I will be here for you."

Tommy smiled. "I am going to tell them I want to stay with you and Uncle Johnny," he said.

"Let's go see if we can find some more birds," Marcie replied. It was a difficult situation and she knew that Tommy had some hard decisions to make. She and Johnny had difficult decisions to of their own to contemplate.

Chapter 16

Johnny heard the sound of a large motor vehicle pulling into the parking lot of the visitor center as he stared at the space in the back of Tommy's dad's pickup where the black lock box was missing. He looked through the side window of the canopy to see the Fielder's motor home pull up next to the curb near the restrooms. Johnny could see Jay Fielder's face through the windshield as he parked the vehicle to cover half a dozen parking spots. He wondered why the man did not take the minor extra effort to pull into one of the larger spaces provided for vehicles that size.

Johnny remained motionless as he heard the engine shutoff and saw Fielder and his wife exit through the large door on the side of their traveling home. Jay was dressed in khaki colored shorts and a maroon golf shirt. He held tightly in his left hand a large clear plastic garbage bag as it blew in the wind. His wife had on light brown designer shorts and a black buttonless blouse with sunglasses and a floppy straw hat with a black sash. She grabbed her hat with one hand as she walked towards the center in the gusty wind.

To his surprise, Johnny watched as the couple removed the lid of the trash can near the phone booth. Jay Fielder dug through the contents of the trash bin dropping aluminum cans into the clear garbage bag his wife held open for him.

Johnny stared in amazement as Fielder replaced the garbage can lid and moved towards the next can at the corner of the visitor center. Were they collecting the cans so they could turn them in at a grocery store and get a deposit refund? Was Fielder's statements about his success in the dot-com market some kind of cover for the level poverty he endured or were the couple some kind of eccentric frugal millionaires trying to keep every dime they earned. Johnny wondered if the couple had hid out all night from the campground in order to avoid paying for a night's rent.

Johnny followed them with his eyes as they walked past the center entrance to the side of the building and the trash can near the Oak Flat Trail trailhead. The building blocked the couple's view of the parking lot and he decided to take the opportunity to exit the vehicle.

He climbed out of the back of the canopy feet first and stood upright on the black asphalt of the parking lot. He carefully closed the canopy door trying not to make a sound, although it probably could not be heard over the roar of the wind blowing debris though the lot. He looked to the east and observed the dark clouds approaching rapidly.

He looked towards the visitor center. The Fiedler's were nowhere in sight. His curiosity got the best of him and he slowly walked towards the log building. He peeked around the corner of the building that the Fielder couple had disappeared behind. They were nowhere in sight. He walked around the building to the railing overlooking the path to the overlook below. There was no sign of the couple on the path or at the overlook. They must have gone down the Oak Flat Trail. A flash of lightning and clap of thunder brought Johnny back to reality. He needed to get back to camp before the storm hit.

Johnny walked down the stone steps from the parking lot to the Rim Rock Trail on the edge of the canyon. He had made a note on his pad about the missing lock-box. He had also taken a picture of the inside of the back of the truck while he was there.

He was unsure of what to do about the missing box. If he told the ranger, he would have to explain what he was doing inside a pickup that was part of an investigation into a death in the park. If he kept it to himself, the investigators may be losing valuable information. He decided to be honest with the ranger when he saw him next, but he would not seek him out either. After all they were all trapped in the park for at least another day. Maybe he could figure out what was going on before he had to report the incident to the authorities.

He continued walking on the dirt path along the rim of the canyon as dark clouds drifted over his head. His thoughts turned to the missing lock-box. Was the box he saw in the Baumgardner's van the same box? If so, what did that mean?

The Baumgardner's certainly had the opportunity to take the box when they were on watch at the visitor center. He had not met Mrs. Baumgardner, but Mr. Baumgardner did not seem like the kind to steal from another person. Johnny had no confidence in his judge of character, so the point about what the man seemed like he was capable of seemed irrelevant. But he also knew that confidence or not, his instincts about people were usually right.

Drops of rain intermittently pelted the dirt on the trail ahead of him. A bright spot of sunshine cast its light through an opening in the low-hanging dark clouds. The light traveled through the air and lit up the walls of the north side of the gorge.

Johnny examined the depth of the canyon ridges as they ran towards the curving river below. He brought his eyes back up to the top of the canyon and looked past the rolling green hills. A mile or so away, a towering column of gray rain reached up to the dark clouds above.

Even if the Baumgardner's had taken the lock-box, did that mean they had anything to do with the death of Tommy's father, Johnny wondered. Baumgardner did not seem strong enough to overpower the dead man, but that was another area in which Johnny had no expertise.

He thought back to when he and Marcie had first arrived at the visitor center before they found the body. Did he really see the Baumgardner's van leaving the area when they first pulled into the lot? So much had happened since then, he could not be sure. If the Baumgardners had been there at that time, they were not there after Johnny and Marcie had found Tommy and stayed in the pickup to escape the thunderstorm. He would have to ask Marcie if she remembered seeing the van in the area.

He thought about the Fielders. What were they doing on the Oak Flat Trail with an impending thunderstorm just a few minutes away? He did not think there were any trash cans on the trail, but the Fielders might not know that. Could they possibly be visiting the scene of the crime? If so, what was the crime and what was their motive?

Method, motive, and opportunity, Johnny thought. He had already established Luke Atkins had opportunity. There was a chance the Baumgardner's were also in the Oak Flat Trail area when the man died, giving them opportunity also. The Fielders claimed to be on the Warner Nature Trail a few miles away at the time of the incident, but they could be lying just as they seemed to be lying about their wealth.

He was still drawing a blank on motive. Even if someone had taken the lock-box from the pickup, they took it long after the man's death; hardly a clear premeditated motive. He had not found anything that connected any of the campers with Tommy and his father.

For method, Johnny suspected strangulation based on his untrained eye's examination of the bruises on the dead man's neck and that there was no trace of blood at the scene. This was all speculation. It was just as likely that the ranger was right and Tommy's father had become disoriented and fell down the cliff. Myerson was right; he should leave the investigation to the professional investigators.

A bright flash of lightning lit up the trail ahead of him and a loud clap of thunder rattled his eardrums. Twenty yards ahead of him on the trail where the lightning had struck, a serviceberry bush burst into flames. A stiff wind fanned the flames on the bush and sparks jumped to the surrounding grass and brush. A wildfire was developing before his eyes.

The sky opened up as he rushed towards the flames. In one motion, he scooped loose dirt with both his hands and threw the dry soil on top of the burning bush. Gray smoke curled its way through the air above the shrub as large drops of rain pounded Johnny's body and the surrounding brush. He covered the bush with two more scoops of dirt and surveyed the surrounding area.

The rain had extinguished the embers in the grass. He walked over the grassy area several times to ensure that no remnants of burning embers remained.

When he was sure the fire was completely out, he ran for cover underneath the nearby oak trees.

As the water began to build up on the trail, he decided he could wait no longer and ran up the muddy path towards camp. Within a few minutes he had reached the familiar black asphalt access road leading into campground Loop C. The asphalt was still dry. He had outrun the isolated shower.

He stood still for a moment trying to catch his breath from the brief physical exertion. When he felt his respiration rate return to normal, he began to walk up the road towards Loop B. He saw the ranger standing at the edge of Luke Atkins' campsite talking calmly to the young man. Johnny waved as he walked past and the two men returned the greeting.

He continued around the loop walking past the Baumgardner's white van. The vehicle sat motionless in the gravel parking spot next to the campsite. He could see the couple sitting around the table in the back of the van, each holding an open book at arms length in front of them. He averted his eyes as he walked by so as to not invade their privacy. He reprimanded himself for being so nosy. People came to campgrounds for peace and solitude and they did not want some strange man peeking through their windows, he thought.

He left the asphalt road and followed the path through the woods to his campsite. He stopped at the edge of the site and looked around. Marcie was sitting in the black canvas chair near the fire pit. Tommy lay across her chest with his arms around her neck. Johnny stood and listened. He could hear a quiet whimpering sound coming from the chair. Tommy was crying.

Johnny slowly approached the couple and observed tears streaming down Marcie's face.

Chapter 17

"You smell smoky and you are all wet," Marcie said as Johnny approached. She sniffled and wiped her nose with a tissue. Tommy stood up off of her and looked at Johnny. His eyes and nose were red and swollen.

"I just put out a wildfire," Johnny said. "Lightning struck a bush on the trail right in front of me. It didn't do too much damage, just threw sparks around the grass. I put them out with some dirt from the trail."

"How are you two doing? You don't look too good, if you don't mind my saying so."

"I think Tommy and I are still sad," Marcie said. Tommy walked over to the log next to the campfire ring, and sat down with his hands between his knees. He looked as if he felt cold; as if he was about to start shivering.

"Being sad is okay," Johnny said. "For a while anyways. Let me change out of these dirty clothes. Maybe I have something to cheer you up."

Johnny walked towards the trailer. As he opened the aluminum door, he observed the Fielder's driving their motor home towards their campsite. He waved at the couple as they drove by but they did not return the greeting. It was hard to tell if they just did not see him or if they were ignoring him on purpose.

He entered the trailer and a few minutes later came out wearing a clean long-sleeved flannel shirt, clean denim pants and sandals. He had in his hands a wooden Native American flute and a silver harmonica. The flute was a cylindrical-shaped mahogany colored piece of wood with a small opening at one end for a mouth piece, six finger-holes on top, and a large opening at the other end.

"They say music calms the savage beast," Johnny said. "I don't know if there are any savage beasts around here or not, but we might as well make some music just in case. Either of you know how to play the flute or the harmonica?"

Both Marcie and Tommy shook their heads in the negative. Johnny could see in their faces that they were wondering what he was up to. Their eyes seemed to have cleared up and their minds were ready to think about something besides the events of the day.

"Before we get started here, why don't you both go wash your faces," Johnny said. "You'll feel better and it will give me a chance to warm up my pipes."

Johnny began playing a song on his Native American flute. He had received the flute as a gift from the State Police officer who had helped comfort him at the time of his wife's death. He had used the flute to pour out his emotions when he had trouble verbalizing deep feelings during times of trouble. Although he had occasionally listened to Native American flute music, he never tried to learn a specific song. He just let the music come out of him, which he understood was how some Native Americans used the flute centuries before the Europeans discovered the New World.

He had read that Native American boys would compose their own individual songs in the solitude of nature. A boy would conceal himself outside his intended love's tipi at night and begin to serenade her with his songs.

Playing the flute was also used as a form of meditation in some tribes. The flute was said to evoke a feeling one might have when on a calming mountain or ocean retreat. In Johnny's judgment the hollow wooden instrument fulfilled its promise every time he played.

As Tommy and Marcie returned to their seats around the campfire ring, Johnny started playing long slow notes through the flute. The notes came to him naturally without any thought. He could feel the release of the natural sound and hoped Marcie and Tommy were feeling it too. He looked over to see the care on the faces of his companions fading into the air. He played on for several minutes with Marcie and Tommy listening with closed eyes. Finally he slowly faded the music and stopped playing.

Marcie and Tommy both opened their eyes and clapped their hands together.

"That was nice," Marcie said. "Very relaxing."

She was very excited with discovering a new side of her friend; a side of him she had not expected to see. She carried Native American flute music in the gift shop next to her restaurant and had occasionally taken a CD home with her to listen to the music. She enjoyed listening to the soothing sounds and used it to help her relax.

Johnny's playing certainly would not win any music awards, but it had a certain heart that was absent from the recorded music she had listened to before. She could feel a warm spot growing inside her chest.

"Do either of you know the story of Kokopelli?" Johnny asked.

Tommy shook his head in the negative.

"Isn't he the Native American flute player," Marcie said. "I've seen drawings of him, but I don't think I know the whole story."

"I read about him some time ago," Johnny said. He lowered his voice and began to tell his story. Tommy leaned towards Johnny and listened intently.

"According to Native American legend, a long time ago there was a humped-backed flute player whose name was Kokopelli. He was a good spirit who talked to the wind and the sky and to the sun and the rain. Every year, after the cold winter season, he traveled across the land with the seeds of plants and flowers in the hump of his back. He helped crops to grow so that everyone had enough food to eat. In the springtime, people listened quietly to hear the sounds of Kokopelli's flute playing. When they heard the music, it brought happiness and joy to their hearts.

"No one knows today what his song was like, but when the Native Americans started making their own flutes they played their own songs and emptied their heart and soul into the flute so the song came out different for everyone who plays."

"Do you want to try to play, Tommy?" Johnny asked.

Tommy nodded his head and walked towards Johnny. As he approached, a mourning dove cooed gently from a nearby oak tree. Marcie recognized the long slow notes coming from the bird as being similar to some of the notes Johnny had played.

"Listen," she said. "The dove is singing. Can you make the flute sound like the dove?"

"I think so," Johnny said. He positioned Tommy so that he was facing away from him and standing in between his legs. "The holes are kind of big, so I'm going to have to help you, Tommy."

After drying the mouthpiece with a paper napkin, he positioned it in front of the boy's mouth.

"I'll cover the holes with my fingers," Johnny said. "So, all you have to do is blow. Take a deep breath and then we'll start playing."

Tommy put his lips over the end of the flute and began to blow. Johnny covered the six holes with his fingers and then alternated lifting his middle finger up and down in rhythm with the mourning dove. Long slow notes flowed from the musical instrument.

Tommy ran out of breath and Johnny told him to keep inhaling through his nose and exhaling through the flute. After a while the boy smiled and looked up at Johnny's face, and Johnny knew that the flute had worked its magic.

"That was very good," Marcie said. "It sounded just like the dove. How did that make you feel, Tommy?"

"Good," Tommy replied. He smiled and walked back to his canvas chair next to Marcie.

"Maybe you two can start a fire," Johnny said. "It'll be dark soon. I'll keep playing so you have some background music. How does that sound?"

"You are very talented," Marcie said. She smiled and Johnny knew her compliment was genuine.

He knew he was not the most talented musician in the world and that he did not play every note perfectly. But, he wanted to help bring peace to Marcie, Tommy and himself and this was the only external tool he had to bring it about. As he took deep breaths and blew through the hollowed out tree limb, he let the vibrations of the sound waves invade his soul.

He wondered what Tommy and Marcie were thinking about as they built a pyramid of kindling over a pile of shredded newspaper. Johnny knew that fire was another soothing element for the human soul and that any kind of activity was brought more peace than sitting around dwelling on something negative. He knew from experience that the worst thing a grieving person could do would be to sit around and wallow in their own sadness all day.

Marcie helped Tommy light a match and ignite the newspaper under the kindling. The two stood by as the flames slowly moved from the outer edges towards the center and then erupted into a pyramid of flames.

Johnny continued to play a haunting melody of a series long drawn out notes with short quick quarter notes between them. Marcie put a small log on top of the kindling and she and Tommy returned to their seats, with Tommy sitting on Marcie's lap on the black canvas chair near Johnny. They stared listlessly into the fire and Johnny wondered if his music was having any affect. Maybe the act of playing, of creating something out of nothing, maybe that was the healing power of the flute, he thought. He stopped playing.

"Keep going," Tommy said. "I like it."

Johnny continued to play until he felt himself getting lightheaded from hyperventilation. He had used the flute for his own personal entertainment, but he had never played for an audience or for as long as his current performance. His body was unaccustomed to the extended breathing exercises.

"I can't go anymore," he said. "I am getting dizzy."

The harmonica was another matter. He could play for hours without taking a break. He set the flute down on the log and picked up the small shiny rectangular instrument. He rubbed it against his lips and blew in and out creating a cacophony of notes. Tommy and Marcie both smiled.

"Do you two know the song *Michael row the boat ashore*?" Johnny asked.

Tommy shook his head, no.

"I do," Marcie said.

"How about a little sing along?" Johnny said. "I'll play the harmonica, Marcie can start singing and you can join in when you've got the words, Tommy."

Johnny began to play the traditional folk song by blowing powerfully through the tiny instrument. At first Marcie just stared at the transformation in the normally quiet and inanimate man she knew. His whole body seemed to wrap itself around the harmonica as he blew with all his might. The notes were tender but exciting; they filled her soul with energy.

"Come on join in," Johnny said after the second chorus and then he started blowing into the instrument again.

"Michael row the boat ashore, halleluiah," Marcie sang quietly into Tommy's ear.

Soon Tommy was lending his voice to the first lines of the song and mouthing the words he did not know. The log on the fire shifted and threw a shower of sparks into the darkening sky; the three companions kept singing softly.

"The river is deep and the river is wide, hallelujah. Milk and honey on the other side, hallelujah," the sounds echoed into the night. They sang several verses and then Johnny raised the silver harmonica above his head.

"I've got to take a break," he said. "I'm all blown out. How about you Tommy, do you know any songs?"

"Old MacDonald," Tommy said.

"Oh, I like that one," Marcie whispered into his ear and squeezed his chest.

"You start us off, Tommy," Johnny said.

Tommy turned his head towards Marcie and blushed.

"Old MacDonald had a farm, E I E I O," Marcie began softly. Tommy and Johnny joined in on the second line.

They continued through several verses allowing Tommy to pick the animal for each stanza until he picked a fish and they could not think of the correct sound to make. All three laughed until their eyes watered.

After they had calmed down for a minute, Johnny said, "Too bad we don't have a guitar and someone who knows how to play."

"At your service," the voice of Ken Myerson came from behind them.

Johnny turned around to see the campground host, guitar in hand, standing next to his wife Louise. He was a little embarrassed at being surprised by strangers during his amateur performance, but Johnny invited the couple into the campsite anyway. He introduced the couple to Marcie and Tommy and offered them a seat on the log next to the campfire ring.

"That was some awful nice singing we heard coming from your site," Ken said. "We thought we might join you if you don't mind."

"As long as you don't pick fish as the animal on the Old MacDonald song," Marcie said. "I think we would love to have you join us. Right, Tommy?"

Tommy nodded his head in the affirmative.

Ken strummed his guitar and said, "Here is a song my daddy taught me."

He strummed the guitar in a gentle rhythm and in a low deep voice began singing, "Oh, give me a home where the buffalo roam; where the deer and the antelope play."

Everyone joined in on the chorus when Ken asked. Tommy and Marcie swayed together in rhythm with the music. "Where seldom is heard a discouraging word; and the skies are not cloudy all day," they sang.

They finished several choruses of the song and then Ken led the group through a few more classic campfire melodies. The camp fell silent as the moon rose in the east. The sound of coyotes howling in the distance wafted through the air.

Johnny offered his guests a soda and passed them each a wet aluminum can from the cooler.

"We were about to roast some hot dogs for dinner," he said. "Care to join us?"

"Louise has some stew in the crock pot we should eat tonight," Ken said. "We should head back soon."

"At least stay until you've finished your soda," Johnny said. "So where are you folks from?"

The group passed the time with idle chit-chat about their lives and discovered that they had much in common. The Myerson's signed up as campground hosts for different parks every year.

"It's a good deal," Ken said. "You get a free camping spot and you get to meet a lot of interesting people. You don't have any official duties except to answer camper's questions and make them feel welcome."

"Ken retired two years ago," Louise said. "We really have enjoyed our life on the road. We have a cabin in Montana we stay at during the winter. We are snowed in for two months out of the year and life just passes us by without us knowing it."

"But, I don't think we can let that stew cook much longer, she said. "We really should be going."

The couple excused themselves and walked slowly out of the campsite to the access road. With his guitar hanging from his shoulder, Ken turned to waved goodbye and then put his arm around his wife as they walked down the road together.

By the light of a lantern Johnny, Marcie and Tommy set the table for dinner and began roasting hot dogs over the fire.

"I like hot dogs, but we should try something else tomorrow," Johnny said. "Maybe I'll plan things better and I can barbeque some hamburgers."

"I took some of the patties out of the freezer," Marcie said. "They should be thawed by tomorrow. I like hot dogs though. How about you Tommy?"

Tommy nodded his head that he did like them.

They finished dinner and Johnny helped Tommy wash up and get dressed for bed. Marcie relaxed by the fire while Johnny tucked Tommy into bed. She could hear Johnny's soft whispers coming from the trailer, but could not make out what he was saying.

"The peregrine falcon can fly at over two hundred miles an hour," Johnny read from Tommy's book on birds inside the trailer. "Its one of the fastest animals on earth."

Just then, a clap of thunder sounded in the distance and rattled the windows of the small travel trailer.

"You know some Native Americans believed that thunder and lightning was caused by a bird like a falcon, only bigger," Johnny said. "They called the bird the Thunderbird and they believed it protected good people from bad people."

"I saw a falcon before my dad got lost," Tommy said.

"I know son," Johnny said. "Maybe the falcon was trying to protect you until me and Aunt Marcie could find you. You know, some people believe that people and animals all have the same spirit inside them. When a person goes away a little piece of that spirit goes into the nearest person or animal that was around at the time they went away."

"Do you think my dad's spirit went into the falcon?" Tommy asked.

"I don't know," Johnny said. "But I do know that you will always have a little piece of your dad and mom's spirit deep inside you. You must always remember that Tommy. Your mom and dad will always be with you."

Tommy closed his eyes and slowly drifted off to sleep while Johnny watched him in silence.

Chapter 18

After he was certain the boy was sound asleep, Johnny turned off the light in the trailer, quietly opened the door and stepped outside. He walked over to the campfire ring and sat down in the black canvas chair next to Marcie. The lantern had been extinguished and the fire was slowly deteriorating into embers. Johnny felt the cool night air against his cheek and looked up at the half-moon rising on the eastern horizon.

"That was an enjoyable evening," he said.

"Yes, it was a lot of fun," Marcie replied. "You really picked up our spirits."

"I shouldn't have left you alone all day like that," Johnny said. "I can't seem to help getting involved when I think something may be overlooked. I need to learn to turn my focus closer to home and stop getting involved in the affairs of others."

"I think you're wrong," Marcie said. "If there is something being overlooked in the death of Tommy's father, then Tommy needs you to stand up for him because he can't stand up for himself. In the long run everyone will be better off. What is it you think is being overlooked?"

"I guess I should wait to see what the investigators say tomorrow," Johnny said. "But, the ranger seems to want to write the incident off as a simple case of a man falling down a cliff to his death.

"However, based on where we found Tommy, I don't think the man was anywhere near the cliff when the boy lost him. I found some evidence that there was a struggle in the bushes near where his dad disappeared. Also, the trail from that area to the top of the cliff looked like it had been swept clean when I examined it this morning. Tommy's father had bruises on his neck and there was no sign of blood like you might expect when someone falls on hard rocks from that height."

"I don't know if there has to be blood," Marcie said. "He could have slid down the embankment and hit his head hard enough to kill him without breaking the skin and bleeding."

"Maybe so," Johnny said. "There are some other things that seem suspicious to me.

"On my walk down to watch the rescue operations, I saw someone in the Baumgardner's van trying to open what looked like the lock-box from the back of Tommy's dad's pickup. I only saw their hands, so I don't know who it was. On my way back tonight, I checked and the lock-box was gone."

"That is strange," Marcie said. "There may be an innocent explanation."

"While I was in the pickup, the Fielders drove up in their motor home," Johnny said. "I told you about them right?"

"You just told me that you went over to their campsite and they didn't seem to be interested in anything but themselves," Marcie said. "You said they claimed to be well off due to the dot-com boon of the nineties."

"You'll never guess what they were doing at the visitor center," Johnny said. "They were digging through the trash bins for aluminum cans and putting them in a garbage bag. I assume they were collecting them so they could turn them in to get a deposit refund. It almost looked as if this was a regular routine for them and that maybe they aren't as well off as they seem to be. Maybe that's why they showed up late and never registered their campsite."

"That is strange," Marcie said. "Maybe they are environmentalists and were just being conscientious and saving any recyclables from going to the nearest landfill."

"They did not seem like the type to me," Johnny said. "After they went through all the cans around the building, they disappeared. I suspect they went down Oak Flat Trail, but I can't figure out why they would, especially I with a massive thunderstorm approaching,"

"Maybe they were looking for more recyclables," Marcie said.

"That could be," Johnny said. "Although I don't think there are any trash cans on Oak Flat Trail.

"By the time I got back from my adventure with the lightning and wildfire, they were already driving into their campsite."

"I almost forgot, I found a gold pin near the bushes with the broken branches at the River Access sign," he said. "The ranger did not even want to look at it. It said *Don't Mess With Texas* and was gold and in the shape of the state of Texas. I took a picture of it; let me get my laptop."

He walked past the trailer to his pickup. He could hear Tommy snoring inside the recreational vehicle. He quietly opened the pickup door, grabbed his laptop, and carefully shut the door. As he walked back to the fire, he stopped and stood still; listening intently. He thought he heard some rustling in the bushes. He looked over towards the Fielder's campsite. The lights were on in their motor home but the shades were pulled down so he could not see inside. After a few seconds he decided that the noise was only his imagination and then moved on.

Marcie had put another log on the fire while he was gone and the flames lit up the area around the ring. Johnny sat down and opened the lid to his laptop. He pulled his camera out of his pocket and connected the cable in the back of the computer to the digital camera. He downloaded the pictures to the computer and then started displaying them one by one on the screen. He moved his chair closer to Marcie's so she could look over his shoulder.

He talked her through the pictures explaining the location of the tennis shoe tracks and the broken branches on the serviceberry bush. He explained about the middle of the trail to the cliff being void of debris while the edges of the trail were lined with twigs and leaves. Marcie rolled her eyes.

"No offense," she said. "But you might be stretching things a little bit there." She wanted to be supportive, but she also felt compelled to be realistic. It was hard to tell whether Johnny was getting carried away with his imagination or whether he was really on to something.

"You may be right," Johnny said. "These next pictures are kind of gruesome, do you want to see them or not?"

"I'll see them," she said. "I just hope they don't give me nightmares."

Johnny flipped to the next two pictures which showed the bubblegum wrapper at the top of the cliff and then the body laying halfway down caught between two rocks. The next pictures showed close ups of the area around the body and the bruises on the man's neck.

"I see what you mean about the bruises," Marcie said. "I hate to say it, but he may have been strangled by something. Could he have hit a tree branch or something else on the way down?"

"I don't think so," Johnny said. "I guess he could have landed on the chain now that you mention it. It's like the Picacho Peak mystery all over again. Was it an accident or foul play?"

"Myerson said that the destruction of serviceberry bush could have been caused by a bear. Could a bear have caused the marks on the man's neck? Or could he have seen the bear and panicked and fell down the embankment hitting branches or the chain along the way?"

"Let's move on to the next picture," Marcie said. She had enough of the sight of a dead man's neck and was sure she would be seeing the image in her sleep that night.

Johnny moved to the next picture and the Texas-shaped gold pin appeared on the screen. Marcie's eyes lit up.

"That looks like the pin that boy with the Volkswagen had in his bandanna," Marcie said.

"Are you sure?" Johnny asked.

"Pretty sure," Marcie said. "Is that important?"

Johnny closed the laptop and set it down on the picnic table. He stood up slowly, threw another log on top of the dwindling fire and surveyed the surrounding area bathed in the light of the campfire. He tried to think of all the possibilities of how a pin matching the one Luke Atkins was wearing could find its way to the area where Tommy had lost his father.

His thoughts were interrupted by the sound of something rustling the bushes in the nearby woods.

He listened intently and the sound went away. He sat back down in his chair.

"Atkins was chewing gum pretty hard when I met him and I found gum wrappers on the Uplands Trail in addition to the one above the cliff," Johnny said. "But he had told me that he never made it down the trail that far. I haven't confirmed that he was chewing the same brand of gum as the wrappers, but I'll bet the investigators can verify that tomorrow. The wrappers and the pin seem like too much of a coincidence."

A loud rustling noise came from the woods. Johnny stood up and listened; there was more rustling. He grabbed the small flashlight he had left on the picnic table. He pointed the light in the direction of the rustling. The rustling suddenly stopped. A large mule deer buck jumped out of the woods, bounded past the campfire and disappeared into the oak forest.

Chapter 19

Johnny Blue tried to make himself comfortable on the small side-couch underneath the table in his fifteen foot travel trailer. He and Marcie had only retired to bed a few minutes earlier, but he felt restless and bored. He wondered what the next day had in store for him. The road out of the park would be open soon and the Park Police investigators would be arriving from their headquarters in Washington, D.C. They would probably be asking him a lot of questions and he wanted to make sure he gave them all the information he could, but he did not want to leave Marcie and Tommy alone like he had during the previous day.

He could hear Tommy snoring next to Marcie on the full bed above him at the rear of the vehicle. He wondered what the future held for the boy. Surely someone from child services would be paying them a visit once the road was open. He wanted to make sure he asked all the right questions to make sure Tommy was provided with good care.

After Tommy had gone to bed, Johnny had told Marcie how he felt. If there was anything he could do about it, the boy would not be entering Colorado's or Arizona's child welfare systems. He wanted to find out his options and start whatever paperwork was required to become the boy's guardian. Marcie seemed to think he was on the right track, but he should take things slowly and make sure he made the right decision for everyone involved.

Joseph A. Mootz

Johnny turned over on the small couch and tried to adjust the blanket over his feet. He was not going to rush in to anything permanent. He knew he was dealing with a boy at a critical age and it would be best to proceed slowly. His instincts told him that barring any unforeseen relative showing up with a good home for Tommy, it would be best for everyone if he could adopt Tommy and raise him as his own.

At the same time his feelings for Marcie were growing. In his mind he saw himself engineering the perfect family and somehow felt guilty about that. Was it guilt over the loss of his first family? Or was it his natural low-self-esteem and self-doubt that questioned his motives? He needed to relax and think positive thoughts about himself. He stared up at the bottom of the wooden cabinets above him and tried to clear his mind.

When he awoke the next morning, the sun was beginning to light up the sky and the local birds had already started their morning chatter. He quietly got out of bed, stepped out of the trailer, and stretched his arms over his head. He put his hand over his mouth and let out a silent yawn. A soft breeze blew the cool morning air against his cheeks as he sat down on the canvas chair near the campfire ring and rubbed his eyes.

His thoughts turned to Luke Atkins. He was convinced that Atkins was lying about a lot of things, but did that mean he had something to do with the death of Tommy's father? It would be best to let the investigators in on what he knew and then let them sort it out, he thought.

It felt good to be out in the quiet morning air. He sat down in his black canvas chair with his feet flat on the ground, his back up straight, and his hands on his knees. He slowly began to breathe in and out clearing his mind of his ego's desires and fears. He let his reasoning go and felt a warm spot growing in his chest. He saw himself walking hand in hand with Tommy on his ranch in the desert. He saw Marcie smiling waiting for them at the front door of his straw-bale house. He continued his regular deep breathing, afraid to break into his mantra for fear of waking up Marcie and Tommy. After a few minutes he felt himself slipping into a deep sense of relaxation.

His peaceful state was suddenly disturbed by the sound of an automobile engine backfiring. He opened his eyes and listened. It sounded as if an unmuffled vehicle was idling in campground Loop C. Johnny continued to listen. He heard a car door slam and the vehicle's engine being revved up. It sounded like the car was moving and getting closer. He peered through the woods that separated his campsite from the Loop C access road and caught a glimpse of Luke Atkins' Volkswagen driving by on the circular asphalt path.

Johnny rushed to his pickup and started the engine. He slowly backed out of his campsite and in his rear view mirror saw the Volkswagen pass by the entrance to Loop B on its way out of the campground. Johnny drove around the loop at a safe speed and tried to understand what he thought he was doing. He was following his instincts. He had no idea why, but he wanted to know what Luke Atkins was up to.

He passed by the Fielder's motor home which was still parked with its shades down. Johnny drove by the campground host's site; Ken Myerson's trailer was dark and no one was outside. He continued driving at a safe pace, made a right turn out of the loop and onto the road that led out of the campground. He passed by the road that led to the ranger's residence. The ranger's trailer was also dark and no one was in sight.

He made another right turn off of the campground access road and onto the park's main road. He saw the vertical chrome tailpipe of the yellow Volkswagen disappear around the corner several hundred yards ahead. Johnny continued slowly driving down the road.

He stopped at the Tomichi Point parking lot on the right side of the road and surveyed the area. The lot was empty. He pulled back on to the road and resumed his steady slow pace under the clear blue morning sky. He rolled down his window and let the cool morning air wash over his face.

He made a right-hand turn into the visitor center parking lot. The lot was empty except for the black pickup belonging to Tommy's deceased father. He drove slowly to the exit and made another right-hand turn back onto the main road. He calmly drove along the narrow winding road looking for signs of the Volkswagen

The pickup and its driver passed by the turnouts for Cross Fissures View, Rock Point, and Devils Lookout. The bug was not in any of the parking spaces marked by the white painted boxes alongside the road. The grade of the uphill road steepened and the frequency of sharp curves increased. When he reached the parking area for the Painted Wall View he could see Atkins' yellow vehicle parked in the parking area next to the tall brown grass along the road.

Johnny parked his pickup behind the bug and looked around. There was no movement from within the vehicle or in the surrounding woods. He opened his door and stepped out into the morning air. He walked slowly towards the yellow bug and peered inside. The vehicle was empty except for candy wrappers and other trash on the passenger seat.

He was very familiar with Painted Wall View. It was one of his favorite stops along the eight mile road that ran along the rim of the canyon. The road had several points for visitors to stop and to see different views of the giant chasm, but Painted Wall was something special.

Johnny knew the dirt path to the viewpoint ran slightly down hill through a small pine and juniper forest. The trail ran as a nearly straight line through the exact center of a hundred foot wide rocky outcropping into the canyon. Small side trails ran through the mountain mahogany bushes and juniper trees to the each edge of the outcropping. At the end of the trail, the rocky structure narrowed to a single point from which one of the most spectacular views of the opposite canyon walls could be seen.

The walls on the other side ran straight up from the bottom of the canyon for fifteen hundred feet to a flat top covered with a dark green pine and juniper forest. The bright pink veins of rock covered the flat dark gray walls running in half circles from the top down to the bottom. A clear view of the muddy river could be seen below piles of dark gray boulders at the bottom of the flat walls.

Johnny continued walking towards the trailhead for the trail that ran to Painted Wall View. The trail was a dirt path through tall brown grass. It immediately rose several feet in elevation over rocky terrain. When he reached the peak of the rise, he could see down the trail to the edge of the canyon. Atkins was walking briskly towards the rim about fifty feet ahead of Johnny.

The trail was lined with mountain mahogany bushes covered with dark green leaves. A twelve foot tall Juniper tree with a dark green spherical-shaped growth of needles stuck on top of its light gray trunk curved into the shape of an "S" stood as a solitary sentinel on the edge of the canyon. Atkins passed underneath the tree as Johnny arrived at the first ridge of the trail. The young man's head was bare and clean shaven. Johnny noticed a red piece of cloth flapping in the man's hand.

"Hey, Luke wait up," Johnny yelled.

Atkins turned around to face him. He stood still for a moment as Johnny waved a friendly hello, then suddenly he took off running towards the edge of the canyon rim. Without thinking, Johnny ran after him.

He ran past the juniper tree keeping his eyes on Atkins as he approached the edge of the rim. He could see Atkins bending over towards the ground. The young man appeared to pick up small stone off the ground.

As he jogged towards Atkins, Johnny kept his eyes on him to see what he was up to. He watched as Atkins hurriedly wrapped the stone in the piece of red cloth and threw them both over the side of the canyon in one motion. The rock flew straight out into the air; the red cloth opened up like a parachute and floated slowly down towards the canyon bottom. His bandana, Johnny thought.

When Johnny caught up with him, Atkins was leaning over the four foot high chain link fence which guarded the canyon rim. The weather worn fence was covered in faded and scratched dark brown paint and was held up by three equally spaced horizontal one inch diameter galvanized steel pipes attached to equally spaced rectangular galvanized steel posts. It ran along the top of a cliff that fell straight down for fifteen hundred feet to the canyon bottom and raging river below. The fence curved around the canyon rim and then abruptly stopped leaving the rest of the rim open for anyone to fall over.

Both men stood slightly bent over trying to catch their breath next to the fence on the edge of the cliff. Johnny stared at the ground below him as he filled his lungs with the thin mountain air. The ground around the fence was made of loose dry dirt and small stones on top of a smooth hard rock surface. A few small mountain mahogany bushes grew up out of the dirt near the canyon rim.

"Why'd you do that?" Johnny asked.

"I didn't do nothing," Atkins replied.

The battle cry of illiterate guilty people, Johnny thought to himself. If he wanted to take the man's statement literally, he would cancel out the double negative and know that he just admitted to doing something.

"I saw you throw your bandana over the side," Johnny said. "Is that what you used to strangle Tommy's father?"

"I don't know what you are talking about," Atkins said. "I didn't strangle anybody and you have no proof I did."

"Getting rid of the bandanna didn't do you any good," Johnny said. "That's not the only evidence they have against you. The medical examiner and police investigators will find out what really happened and you will be in a lot of trouble."

"I heard you talking about me around the campfire last night," Atkins said. "I know what you think, but I ain't going to be hassled for something I didn't do."

"So what?" Johnny said. "You just want me to tell them I didn't see you throw the bandana you strangled him with over the edge of the canyon."

"I didn't strangle anyone and you can't prove I did," Atkins said.

He swung his fist at Johnny's head. Johnny jerked his head and shoulders back and the fist just grazed his nose. He lost his balance and fell backwards over a boulder. Atkins took off running up the trail towards the parked vehicles.

Johnny felt himself slipping towards the unguarded edge of the canyon rim. His feet passed over the edge and he continued to slip down over the loose gravel on the hard rocky surface. He grasped at the loose dirt on top of the smooth hard rock but could not find a hand hold.

He continued to slowly slip over the edge of the cliff. His legs dangled fully over the side and he felt his body picking up speed as it slid downward. In one violent motion, he managed to roll himself on to his side and reach out with his arms. He grabbed the edge of the metal post at the end of the fence around the canyon rim and held on as he heard rocks bouncing down the canyon wall below him.

Chapter 20

Johnny tried to calm himself as he held on for his life. He took several long deep breaths as he felt the sharp edge of the metal post dig into his fingertips. He used every ounce of strength he had to pull the upper part of his body over the edge of the cliff and then managed to dig his elbows into the solid rock floor. A few seconds later he had pulled himself completely to safety.

He bent over the metal fence trying to catch his breath. His fingers and arms were bleeding from grasping at the hard ground while trying to save his life. He looked over the edge and stared down at the fifteen hundred foot drop he nearly experienced for himself first hand.

The sound of Atkins' Volkswagen engine interrupted his thoughts. He turned to run up the trail towards his truck. As he neared the end of the trail, he could hear the bug driving down the park access road back the way it had come. Within a few minutes he approached his pickup which was waiting for him exactly as he had left it.

He started the truck's engine, made a U-turn and followed after Atkins. As he traveled down the curvy narrow road, he drove faster than he would have liked but still took the sharp corners at what he thought was a safe speed. He did not think Atkins had anywhere to go. It would not do anyone any good if he ran his truck off the road, he thought as he rounded a particularly sharp corner. He passed by the visitor center and Tomichi Point. There was no sign of the Atkins' vehicle. When he reached the long straight stretch before the entrance to the campground, the vehicle with the vertical tailpipe was still nowhere in sight.

He had to decide whether to continue his search in the campground on his left, drive to the blocked exit to the park on his right or continue straight ahead to East Portal Road. The decision was soon made for him. The Volkswagen pulled onto East Portal Road from the park exit road right in front of Johnny's pickup. Without questioning his actions, Johnny followed the chrome tailpipe down the steep winding road.

He slowed down to let Atkins pull ahead so as to not put pressure on him to make a mistake and possibly run off the road and slide down the steep canyon walls. He had no interest in harming Atkins. He just wanted to make sure that if he did commit the crime that he turned himself in to the proper authorities.

Johnny focused on his own driving. His older model pickup had considerable play in its steering wheel making it difficult to navigate the sharp steep corners of the narrow road. He slowed the pickup down to a crawl using the lowest gear he had and lost sight of the Volkswagen ahead of him.

He tried to think about what he was going to do when he got to the bottom of the canyon. The road dead ended at the river except for the small campground to the left. All he wanted to do was to contain Atkins and make sure he did not get away. The only option he could think of was to block the man's exit and hope he gave himself up peacefully.

He reached the bottom of the steep road and observed the Volkswagen parked near the river's edge. The entrance to the campground was blocked by a closed metal gate. Johnny swerved his pickup around and drove it back and forth until it exactly blocked both lanes of the road. A sharp drop off in front of the vehicle and a steep canyon wall behind it prevented Atkins from trying to escape.

Johnny stepped out of his pickup and walked to the front of the vehicle. The sound of the rushing water from the river nearly drowned out the sound of the Volkswagen's engine as it sat idling with Luke Atkins behind the steering wheel. Suddenly the engine shut off and Atkins stepped out of his car.

Johnny walked slowly towards him with his hand in a gesture that indicated he meant no harm to the young man. Atkins circled around to the front of his vehicle and turned towards the river with his back to Johnny.

"Hold up Luke," Johnny yelled. He quickened his pace towards the man. "It's probably not as bad as you think. Why don't we talk about it?"

Suddenly Atkins stripped off his shirt and ran towards the water. He slipped and fell down on the smooth rocks near the shore, stood back up and then dove out into the raging current. Johnny yelled after him as his head bobbed up and down in the white water.

He ran along the shore yelling at the man floating quickly downstream. He looked around for a rope or tree branch with which to try to save him. Out of the corner of his eye, he caught the image of Ranger Harrison Dodge and Ken Myerson running from Myerson's truck towards the river. The truck was parked behind Johnny's pickup which still blocked the road.

The ranger ran down the shoreline with a rope in his hand. Myerson and Johnny fell in close behind him. They reached the bend in the river at the edge of the campground. The ranger jumped in the water up to his ankles. Atkins came floating down the stream with his hand outstretched and his mouth open. The ranger threw the end of the rope and it landed directly downstream from the flailing man. Atkins grabbed the rope as his body floated over it. The ranger pulled the rope taut and Atkins appeared to go limp in the water. Johnny and Myerson jumped into the shallow water near the shore and helped the ranger pull the man to shore.

When Atkins reached the shallow water near the river bank, Myerson and Johnny grabbed him underneath his arms and dragged him on to a dry flat area in the campground parking lot. Atkins lay on his back breathing hard while the three other men stood around him, breathing just as heavy.

"What the hell is this all about?" the ranger said to Johnny.

Johnny relayed the story of the morning's activities and the information about the origin of the pin they had found on the trail. He explained as best he could his conviction that Atkins had killed Tommy's father and hid him in the bushes where he had found the broken serviceberry bush. When circumstances prevented him from leaving the park, he panicked and tried to make it look like an accident by throwing the body down the steep embankment while he was supposed to be on watch for the man to return.

"Is this true?" the ranger asked Atkins.

"He turned my mother against me and then he killed her," Atkins said. He was still out of breath and his words came out in short gasps. He had turned over on his side, coughed and spit out some of the river water he had swallowed.

"Who did?" the ranger asked.

"Tom Atkinson," Atkins said. "He stole my mother away from my father when I was six and then he moved her to Arizona so I couldn't see her. I hadn't seen her for more than ten years and then I got a call that she was dying of cancer. I went to the hospital and the bastard was sitting there chain-smoking in the waiting room right in front of me and his kid. That's when I knew he had killed her. He had given her cancer with all his smoking and she died from it.

"I followed him around for the last couple of months after she died and found out he was coming up here for vacation. Spending the insurance money he got for killing my mother; money that should have been mine. I saw him park his truck at the visitor center and knew he'd be coming down Oak Flat Trail, so I waited for him."

"I didn't want to hurt the kid," Atkins continued. "Luckily he fell behind just where I was waiting. I strangled the bastard with my bandanna, threw him in the bushes, and got the hell out of there before the kid came looking for him."

"You jerk," Johnny said. "Do you know what you did to that boy making him an orphan? Do you know what would have happened to him if he had gone a little farther down the trail and found his father dead in the bushes?"

"No worse than what that bastard did to me," Atkins said.

"Yeah well there are better ways to handle problems like that," Johnny said. He was livid over the arrogance and unapologetic attitude of the man. The boy had not learned that two wrongs do not make a right and now little Tommy would be the one to pay for his ignorance.

"You are just lucky Marcie woke up Myerson after Johnny went after you," the ranger said.

He took out a plastic zip-tie from a pouch on his belt and used it to handcuff Atkins' hands behind his back. "If they hadn't got me up and we hadn't have come along with a rope when we did, your head would have been smashed to a million pieces in that river right now."

"Thanks for nothing," Atkins said.

Chapter 21

After further interrogation by the Park Service Investigators, Atkins confessed to taking the lock-box from the back of the black pickup. He thought he would find money to take as reparations for the loss of his mother. When he broke it open all he found was personal items and pictures of his mother and her other family and he regretted taking it. He took the small amount of money that was in the box and some pictures of his mother. Then he hid the security container in the Baumgardner's van when they were away. He thought that if he became a suspect, he might be able to confuse the issue long enough for him to get away by framing the Baumgardner's.

The Park Service investigators questioned Johnny extensively. He answered their questions honestly and openly and for that they were grateful. They collected the evidence he directed them to, including the bubblegum wrapper, Texas pin, photographs of the scene, and the pieces of paper he used to mark the spot where he had found Tommy. Atkins had admitted moving the pieces of paper in another attempt to confuse the investigation.

The black pickup owned by Tommy's father and the stolen lock-box were impounded as evidence in the case against Atkins who was charged with murder and theft. The investigators allowed Johnny to retrieve several personal items belonging to Tommy including his sleeping bag, pillow, plastic wallet and pictures of him with his parents from the pickup and the lock-box.

The road to the park was opened late the next day. It had been temporarily repaired by installation of a large culvert covered with boulders, fill dirt and gravel. Plans were made to permanently repair the road before the winter season arrived with its drifts of snow, snowmobiles, and cross country skiers.

A representative of Colorado Child Protective Services arrived to see to Tommy's needs. After several long discussions with Tommy, Marcie, and Johnny both individually and as a group, the social worker agreed to allow Tommy to stay with the couple until she could do background checks on them and check with the Arizona Division of Children, Youth and Families. It would be up to the directors at the state level to determine whether Johnny and Marcie could be assigned as temporary guardians until a permanent solution could be found.

After a few days the social worker returned with papers for Johnny and Marcie to sign. They were to report to the Tucson office of the Pima County Department of Health and Human Services when they arrived back home. They both signed their names on the document assigning them temporary joint custody of Tommy.

Exactly one week after arriving in the park, the trio took one last hike around the canyon rim and stopped by the visitor center. Tommy bought a small plastic replica of a serviceberry bush flower with money from his plastic wallet. As they walked out of the visitor center they passed by the Oak Flat Trail trailhead sign. To their surprise a peregrine falcon was perched on a small oak tree just above the wooden plaque.

Tommy broke away from Johnny and Marcie and ran to the sign. He placed the plastic flower in a crack on the post holding up the wooden marker.

"Good bye daddy," he said. "I'll miss you, but I know God will take care of you."

The falcon gracefully flew away with its powerful wings. The sound of thunder in the distance echoed through the canyon as the mighty bird floated on the wind currents above it.

Chapter 22

"This feels right," Johnny said to Marcie as he helped her step into the railroad passenger car.

They were in Durango, Colorado about to take a ride on the Durango and Silverton Narrow Gauge Railroad. They had stayed the night in one of the local campgrounds and had gotten up early to catch the train so they would be back in time to camp outside of Gallup on their way back to Tucson. Tommy had run ahead in the railroad car and was climbing over the worn seats and hanging his head down below them to see what was underneath.

"What feels right, this old train?" Marcie said.

"No, us," Johnny said. "Us three, it feels right, don't you think?"

"Yes, Tommy is a wonderful boy," Marcie said. "He's been through a lot, but he has not lost his curiosity about the world."

The two sat down in a seat at the rear of the car as other passengers filed in. Tommy waved at them from a seat at the front of the car.

"What about you and I," Johnny said. "How does that feel to you?"

"You know when my first husband died, I never thought I'd get over it," Marcie said. "We were soul mates. We used to finish each other's thoughts without ever saying a word. I was lost without him.

"Those first few years alone were difficult. I found myself questioning my every move. I was afraid to change; afraid to think about the future; afraid to dare to want anything that I did not already have."

"And now?" Johnny said.

"And now," Marcie said. "I'm ready. I'm ready to start wanting again; ready to live again.

"What would it be like, us three together?"

"That's a loaded question," Johnny said. He put one arm around her shoulders and rested the other on her leg as the railroad car jerked into motion. Tommy was kneeling on the seat at the front of the car and staring out the window.

"I see us married, living in a straw-bale house on a small ranch in the middle of the desert," Johnny said. "I see us picking up Tommy at school and taking him to baseball and soccer practice. I see us sitting out on the porch at night sipping on lemonade or iced tea and eating homemade ice cream."

"But how will we occupy our time during the day?" Marcie asked. "Will we have friends or will we be a family of hermits?"

"I guess I hadn't thought that out," Johnny said. "It sounds like I was trying to bring you two into my own original idea to hide from the world. That's not what I want. I'm through hiding.

"How about this, I see me selling my land and you selling your house and restaurant. We'll buy a motor home and travel the world. We'll home-school Tommy as we travel."

"I'm serious," Marcie said. "I like the part about starting over, but Tommy is going to need structure. He's going to need to have friends and things to do.

"You know when he is eighteen you will be sixty seven. Have you thought about that?"

"And you will still be in your early forties," Johnny said. He smiled and squeezed her neck with his arm. "I don't see that as a problem. I was fortunate to retire early in life and I think that will keep me active much longer."

They each silently stared ahead listening to the rhythmic sounds of the train passing over the steel tracks. Both of them felt very comfortable and neither would characterize the pause as an awkward silence.

"You're right," Johnny said. "Okay, we sell your house, keep my ranch and your restaurant, but we still buy the motor home and every summer we close the restaurant and travel across the United States."

"I might be able to live with that," Marcie said with a smile. "We'll have to get some horses and find kids to come out and play with Tommy on the weekends."

Darkness encompassed them as the train passed through a tunnel. Johnny pulled Marcie's head towards him and kissed her passionately until the light returned.

"Will you marry me?" Johnny said.

Marcie pulled back slightly, smiled, and turned her face towards the window away from Johnny.

"I need to think about it," she said. "I'll let you know when we get back to Tucson."

She turned her face back towards him, smiled and brushed his cheek with her hand.

"You are a good man, Johnny Blue," she said.

Tommy came running down the aisle between the seats and jumped on to their laps laughing and smiling.

Order the complete Johnny Blue Mysteries

Follow the adventures of Johnny Blue as he travels America's campgrounds solving mysteries and living the dream

Fill out the form below and mail with your check or money order to:

Living the Dream Publishing
PMB 173
8340 N Thornydale #110
Tucson, Arizona 85741

Product	Price	Quantity	Total
Picacho Peak Mystery	$14.95		
Black Canyon Mystery	$14.95		
Melting Glaciers Mystery (Coming in Fall of 2004)	$14.95		
		Total	

Ship To:

Contact Information

Name: _____

Phone: _____

Email: _____

The Johnny Blue Mystery Series
Follow the adventures of Johnny Blue as he travels America's campgrounds solving mysteries and living the dream.

Picacho Peak Mystery
Johnny Blue investigates the mysterious deaths of a young couple in Picacho Peak State Park and suspicious blue crystals near an aqueduct in southern Arizona.

Black Canyon Mystery
Johnny Blue and his close friend Marcie solve the mystery behind a lost boy in Black Canyon of the Gunnison National Park in Colorado.

COMING SOON!

Melting Glaciers Mystery
Johnny and Marcie put themselves in harm's way to solve the mystery behind drownings in Glacier National Park in Montana.

Orders and Information
www.livingthedreampublishing.com

Living the Dream Publishing
PMB 173
8340 N Thornydale #110
Tucson, Arizona 85741